DARKNESS UNBOUND

To the fairest…

Table of Contents

PREFACE

Here we are again. At the beginning of a book, it is generally accepted that the author say something about the body of work that follows, but I can't think of a thing to say. I could tell you about the countless hours of writing and rewriting that have been put into this, or I could tell you about how some of these stories kept me up at night, but in the end, you have bought the book and that's what matters. You came back for more. That is the thing that I want to write about.

I don't write these things for myself, I do it for you. If I want something for myself, I will pick up something from a bookstore and *read*, not write. I will go see whatever box office smash hit that is playing at my local theater. I will look for input, not output. The only part of me that does this for any kind of selfish reasons is that little bit of darkness that everyone has within them. The small part of your mind that wonders what is really around the dark corner or what is *really* creeping about in the abandoned house down the block. That part of me wants to get out from time to time and stretch its tentacles. It wants to reach across time and space and touch that darkness within you, the reader, and communicate the weird things it molds within its mental cage. It can become addicting. Trust me, I know this.

So, once again, I find myself with a darkness that has been let off its leash to stalk through these pages and seek out the scary little corners of your mind. But I warn you, don't let it stay. When you are done, go outside and enjoy the light. Be at peace in the day. Take in the sun. I say this because, when all is said and done, the dark is right there on its heels, ready to spread over everything and make good use of its time.

1

Tyler D. Hansen
Saint Paul, MN
5/30/2013

BANDAGED

He sat in the basement apartment alone, at least in the sense that there were no other *people*. The others were always there. In fact, he couldn't remember a time when they weren't there. He couldn't remember his life before, if there was a before at all. No, there was, he just had no memory of it, or who he was in that life. He knew there was a name he had been called then, but they had taken that from him, along with everything else. Everything, that is, except his blood. His blood stayed where it was until it needed to be let out.

The woman was the first, he remembered that, but he couldn't remember what was happening before she rode him. The sensation was all that came to mind. The feeling of being penetrated by something not human. His skin being filled up with something that wasn't him. It was the sensation of being worn. He remembered that first night, and how she had taken his body to fulfill her lust. Women, men, it didn't matter. She just wanted sensation, and that's what he provided her with. She was essence and he was flesh. He couldn't stop her, so that first night, trapped in his mind and looking out through his own eyes as if it weren't him at all, he wept.

Then came the man. The man was much bigger than he was, and his appetite for pain was overwhelming. He just wanted to hurt something, and he didn't care how. Stray cats, homeless people, and unassuming children were his favorite. A blade was too easy for him. It had to be barbed wire. Small cuts that bled and bled. When they passed out from the pain, the man would wake them up. And again, he sat trapped behind the windows that his eyes had become. He would scream, but none of them would listen. Not the lustful woman and not the savage man.

The little girl made him cry as she would walk in his skin, just wanting to belong. Parents would rush their children from the playgrounds and the child would retreat, leaving him, half in and half out of his mind, to ramble to the police that would show. They did nothing, because he did nothing. The little girl just wanted a friend. The police would tell him to move along and that a playground was no place for a grown man to be lurking about. They would leave, and the child would come back. He thanked God it was never the savage man that came back instead.

It was only when he found the box cutter that he found freedom. When they would begin scratching at his mind, he would cut his arm. They would flee, knowing full well that harm caused to their precious vessel was not a good thing. How could they fulfill their desires if the man-suit they wore was broken? They couldn't. So he threatened himself. He cut. And cut. And cut.

After that, the three became more. At first, five. Then ten. Then twenty-five. They nipped at his mind like dogs on the heels of someone carrying the food they craved. They never moved to take him while he was awake. They waited until he slept. Sometimes, he would awaken in strange places, performing strange acts. Some sexual, some bloody, some kind. It was a mixed bag of where he would end up. Sleep became a problem. He couldn't bleed if he was asleep. He couldn't lock himself in the basement apartment, because they would simply unlock whatever he set up. He had to trap himself.

Restraining himself was difficult. He had no desire to die. Quite the opposite in fact. He wanted to live, and he wanted it to be peaceful. But if he shackled himself and threw the key where he could not reach, starvation would set in, along with dehydration. No, dying wasn't an option. Bleeding, sure, but not dying.

He remembered laughing as the simple solution of swallowing the key came into mind. Swallow that, and then muscle relaxers. Even if they took him as he slept, they wouldn't be able to move, let alone sift through shit to retrieve the small silver key. That didn't stop them from trying. He could feel the aches and see the marks on his wrists where the restraints dug in. And the sleep was never restful. In his dreams, he felt the rage of the savage man and the yearning of the lustful woman. He also felt the terror of the murdered teen and the hatred of the wrathful bigot. Sometimes the sad little girl came through, and those times, as sad as they were, granted him the release of not waking up with bile in his throat or cum in his pants.

But still, during the daylight hours, he would cut to keep them at bay. His secret of not actually wanting to die stayed a secret, but measures had to be taken. He had to start cutting deeper, or in places that would shock even the most perverted of them. His chest and his arms were filled with jagged scars, and his legs throbbed because of the deep gouges. Eventually, clothes hurt too much. On one of his last outings beyond the apartment, he had almost passed out from the pain. It was then, he remembered thinking, he should never leave again.

He set up deliveries for food and drugs to come right to his apartment door. It disgusted him to use the money he had gathered from the people the savage man had tortured and killed, but it was necessary if he were to save the world from himself. His muscle relaxers became hard to come by, but he managed to fake the proper documentation. How? How had he done that, he thought. It was from before.

Something with a pad and a pen and a knife. Was he a doctor? It made sense if he was. He had shed any identification after the savage man took his first victim. He didn't want to be linked in any way to the things the savage man had done, even if it was his body. His skin.

Yes! A doctor! It was how he cut so skillfully with the box cutter that now looked rusted with the color of dried blood and viscera. He sat there in his ragged and bloody bandages and smiled. He remembered. It made sense now. He could remember nothing else, but he knew he had been…no…he *was* a doctor; a man who dealt in the absolutes of life and death. He had saved lives before. Now, he was a scarred shell, but at one point he had decided to dedicate his life to helping people.

The murderous teen crept in as his revelation distracted him, but he knew better. He lunged for the box cutter and slashed at his face. The pain came, but he blocked it out, turning his attention to the intruder. The murderous teen receded, and he could almost hear the others chiding the interloper for trying to fuck with him while he was conscious. He too let out a throated laugh, coughing as he did. He couldn't remember the last time he had made any kind of sound. He certainly hadn't spoken in a while, and the thought that he may have forgotten how both amused and saddened him.

The day stretched on, and his mind kept repeating the same phrase to him.

"I'm a doctor," it said.

This brought him a level of elation he hadn't thought possible anymore. A thought that he could find more evidence of his past life somewhere in the apartment turned up nothing, but that hardly mattered to him. For a while, the sadness of forgetting his own name even fled. But questions arose as he thought. How had he gotten to the apartment? Was it in his name? The groceries and the drugs that were dropped off weren't addressed to him. That much he knew. They didn't have the ring that he knew his own name would have. He was not Bradley Richardson. He was not Janet Van Dyke. He was…

"Doctor," he said. It surprised him to hear the sound of his own voice. He wondered if he could say something else, but decided not to chance it. How long had it been since he had spoken? The question spawned hundreds of others, some old, some new. But it was not the time for questions. He now had something he hadn't mere moments ago. He had a voice, and he had a purpose. There was very little else that mattered now. For the first time in months, or what he came to think of as months, he saw a light in the darkness his existence had been mutated into.

He rushed to the bathroom and looked for pieces of the mirror that the savage man had shattered long ago. If there were any, maybe seeing his own face could unlock more of who he had been. A feeling of excitement came over him. He had an identity, now he wanted to put a face to it, and maybe a name. A name would have been glorious. Something besides "shell" or "skin". A few of the others just called him "meat".

Something shiny caught his attention from under the sink. Just where the base of the porcelain tower had come away from the floor, a piece of the broken mirror jutted out. He lunged for it and the piece stabbed into his hand. He didn't feel it. His adrenaline was too high with the promise of a face. New blood mixed with the old that had stained the floor. It made his fingers slick as he carefully removed the sliver, but he managed to pluck it from the crevice with the grace of a surgeon. The thought made him laugh again. Perhaps that's what he was.

It wasn't big enough for him to glimpse his entire face in its reflective side. He tore the gauze bandages from his face and examined each feature closely. His nose, his mouth, and each scar that he had carved; each one seemed alien to him, as if it wasn't his. Then he stared into his own eye. It was a steel blue eye flecked with green around the pupil. *That* was his. He knew it. For thirty years he had looked at those eyes in the mirror each morning.

Thirty

The number rang out in his head. He was thirty years old. Or he had been when the nightmare he was living in began. He remembered a group of people all telling him "Happy birthday!"

"It's all downhill from here," Marcus had said to him.

"Drink this!" Peter had said, shoving a shot of a brown liquid into his hand.

"I love you, honey. Happy birthday," Amber had said.

Amber

He remembered her. He remembered her black hair and her dark brown, almost black eyes. He remembered the banner she had hung up in the bar.

HAPPY 30TH SAM

That was his name.

"Sam," he croaked. The others became frenzied at the utterance and began tearing at his mind. He screamed and grabbed at the sides of his head. There was nothing he could do to stop it. He could feel his own consciousness being pushed aside to make room for all the other minds crawling over each other to be the first to crush whatever thoughts had tumbled into the light.

The sliver of mirror

Sam reached out and took the shard in his hand. He screamed with everything he had and planted it into his right eye. The others retreated, horrified. His mind was his once again, but he could feel the dripping gore running down his face. One of the eyes that had opened his mind was now no more than a popped grape rolling around in his skull. One window to his true identity was shattered. Sam began to laugh until he cried.

Hours passed and Sam lay on the floor of the bathroom. He tried to move a few times, but he slipped on the tiles now covered in sweat and blood. He gave up for the moment and decided to simply contemplate while he could. The others played at the edge of his mind, but such an extreme act had them afraid of what he might do next should they cross through. The thought that for once they were afraid of him pleased him, and he smiled.

His name was Sam and he had been a doctor. He had a girlfriend or a wife named Amber who loved him very much. He was around thirty years old, and somehow he had managed to cover his existence in the basement apartment from everyone. He had facts to cling to, and in the horror that his life had become, these were bright lights that gave warmth and comfort. Questions still remained unanswered, but he didn't care. The facts were what mattered.

"Do you want to see?" said a voice. It was the little girl. Through the pain and the murmurs of all the rest, the little girl's voice rang out clearly in his mind.

"See?" he asked.

"Do you want to see?" she repeated. Sam didn't know how to respond. He didn't know what the little girl was planning, but he never knew what any of them really wanted. He only knew the outcome of their trips in his skin.

"Yes," he said. "I want to see."

11

Sam felt the little girl creep into his mind. He let her come, and felt her small essence fill him up. This time, however, everything was different. It wasn't her taking control. It was more like a pairing of the two minds. He felt it was akin to being a passenger in his own car as opposed to being forced out and locked in the trunk. He relaxed and waited.

The memories that played out were not his own. They were through the eyes of the little girl. She stared up at the bright lights and dark figures moved around her. The smell of blood and antiseptic filled her nostrils, and that only brought about more panic. One figure moved close to her, then came into vision clearly.

"It's alright. We're going to make sure it doesn't hurt anymore," he said. The little girl tried to speak, but the figure placed a mask to her mouth and nose. She began to drift and her vision became blurred, almost as if she was looking at everything through a thin film of water. The only thing she could make out was the figure. He had a tight fitting blue hat on, and a mask covering his mouth. The only thing she could see was his eyes. His steel blue eyes.

The memory faded to black. The little girl left Sam's skin and went back to the edge.

"That was…you…a-and me?" he asked.

"Do you see?" she asked. Sam had no idea what she wanted him to see. What he could tell from the memory was that she had been injured, and he had been her doctor, then blackness. The memory ended. Or was it that she…

"You died?" he asked.

"Yes," she said. The small revelation added nothing to the big picture Sam had been piecing together all day. He became angry.

"So what?! You died! People die every day! If I knew…if I could remember…I'm sure I lost more than a few people!"

Twenty-five

Sam fell silent.

"Now you see," said the little girl. With that, they all came. One by one, they took him and showed him their final moments, and the last vision they saw was Sam. Each one had believed him when he said they would be alright. Each one had never awoken again. Sam didn't fight them. He let their memories play out, and with each one, his own came back.

The sense a doctor can get when dealing with patients so close to the brink of death can be a powerful thing. Sam had felt that power. A sense of God-like entitlement that rang out in his heart. He could let them slip away, or he could save them. It was his decision. His colleagues sang his praises, as did his parents. His girlfriend validated his ego by screaming in pleasure as he fucked her every night. He lived in a condo that put everyone he knew to shame. He drove a new car every year. He was smart, capable, good-looking, and physically perfect.

It was at his peak that he had decided to begin judging them. He felt like shit allowing the dregs of humanity the precious gift of life when he knew they would just turn around and keep sucking the soul out of everyone else. How could he allow criminals, junkies, and the hopelessly lost to continue on with their miserable lives? He had the power to cleanse the Earth of as many of them as he could get his hands on, and he knew that he would never get caught. He was too smart to get caught.

The little girl had been the last. She had been hit by a car on the worst side of town, and was pretty banged up.

13

Sam felt sorry for her and knew that if he saved her, she would go through life paralyzed from the waist down. In fact, he wasn't sure he could save her at all. Instead, he put her under and nicked a vital artery during surgery. Her insides were already mashed, so it wasn't hard to disguise what he had done. She bled to death quietly, and Sam considered what he had done to be an act of mercy. He had saved that little girl from the worst life she could have had.

The others were taking him because he had chosen to deny them life. He owed them their sick pleasures and horrible acts. He owed them their wretched existence. They were taking it back, or what little they could, by force.

Finally alone in his own mind, Sam vomited bile and blood all over the bathroom floor. His head spun and his thoughts became disjointed. He felt the grip of unconsciousness tightening. He slipped and scrambled to get to his shackles. No matter what they believed he owed them, he would not give in to their wishes. He was better than them and he knew it down to his core. Even scarred and bandaged and now blind in one eye, he was better than they had ever been.

Sam reached his shackles and locked them into place around his wrists and ankles. He reached the muscle tranquilizers and swallowed five of them in a single gulp. With all his precautions taken, he laid back and let sleep begin to take him. The mangled orb that had been his eye pulsed with pain, but he didn't care. He had won another night. His memories were restored, and they were kept at bay until he could get to the key in the…

The key

He had forgotten to swallow the key. Sam sat up, looking for it. He jerked around in his chains as best he could, but the muscle relaxers were already taking effect. He

14

began to panic. Where was it? He had retrieved it in the morning and had taken it to the sink to wash it off.

Sam looked over and saw they key sitting next to the kitchen sink on the other side of the apartment. His heart sank. He was locked in place, his consciousness fading, and there was no way to get to it. On the edge of his mind, the others howled with laughter. Again, the little girl's voice came.

"It's alright," she said.

Sam screamed until he passed out.

DAE

"She's a bomb, Zero," said The Hessian. "She's a four-foot psychoactive volcano, and I'm stating for the record that if you don't get her out of here, I'm gone."

Zero sat in the dark cavern. The one bare bulb above the table faded, and then surged. The generators had been going haywire since the cold season hit, but the mechanics said it would pass. That wasn't Zero's concern at the moment. He had bigger problems, namely, the oversized mercenary sitting across the table from him claiming the girl they had risked their skins for was some kind of psych-bomb. He couldn't lose The Hessian. The man and his subordinates had joined Indigo Group a little less than a season ago, and their help had been invaluable on the last few outings.

"What would you have me do? Send her back? Have her walk across the Blast just to be put back in a tank? And if she is some kind of human psych-bomb, wouldn't it be better for us if she was on our side?" Zero asked.

"They could still be monitoring her. You said it yourself—the intel on the job came out of nowhere. Some Indigo Group on the other side of the country. Had you even heard of Prophet's Grace before then?"

"No, but there are new Groups forming all the time. Every time there is an escape, the refugees have the choice of going nomad or sacking up and joining us," Zero replied. He knew all too well what escaping into the Blast was like. He had done exactly that several years ago. Zero spent those years since learning how to survive in the Blast, making a home of the uninhabitable glass fields and dust deserts, and at the same time, fighting for his life with Indigo Group.

"You should know, better than anyone, just how devious and twisted the DHE can be. I mean, how long did you live in a City? You've seen the Blanks, the kidnappings, the experiments. Anything that comes out of a DHE lab is a weapon. They control everything, and what they can't control, they kill and clone. Send her away, Zero," said The Hessian.

"I can't send a child to die in the Blast." Zero looked the man dead in the eye, showing him that the decision to keep Dae was final. The Hessian stood, staring right back at Zero. He leaned across the table.

"I can, especially when she's just another soulless Blank." The two men stared hard at each other, neither one moving an inch. Zero knew The Hessian was as serious about banishing Dae as he was about keeping her. The Hessian turned to leave, but Zero spoke.

"Let Vice do her thing on her. If she folds, then you're square to do what you want. But if she passes, she stays. Can you agree to that?" The Hessian stopped, looking over his shoulder.

"I don't trust Visionaries, Zero," he said.

"I know, but you trust me. And I trust Vice. That's gotta mean something," said Zero. He had known men like The Hessian before. Trust was the only thing that mattered when you were roaming the Blast. And Indigo Group letting him and his men in had taken a lot of trust, on both sides.

"I do trust you, Zero. So I'll let your girl do her thing," he replied. The Hessian turned and looked at Zero from the doorway. "You're a good leader, but you don't have the stomach for war."

"It's not a war. It's survival," said Zero.

***

18

"Just relax, Dae. Vice here is just going to make sure you're alright. Did you ever get a med-scan back in the City?" asked Zero.

"I've never been to the City," said the little girl. Zero had nurtured his ability to read people. It was an ability that came in handy more often than not when navigating the Blast. You meet a nomad who seems nice enough, but in the night he makes off with a few B-packs and some rations, possibly killing a few people in the process. You *had* to know how to read people. Nice wasn't an option with strangers. And he could tell that the little girl in the chair next to him was scared out of her mind.

Across from Dae sat a dark-skinned woman. Four scars ran across her left cheek, streaks of light against her complexion. She was dressed in a slight variation of the uniform of Indigo Group. Where there should have been the purple crescent moon on her left breast, there was instead a blue eye. The symbol of a Visionary, not a soldier.

"Are you ready, child?" asked Vice.

"She's ready," said Zero. Vice raised an eyebrow, looking at him.

"I didn't ask you, did I?" she said. Zero half smiled and turned to leave. Dae grabbed his wrist.

"Stay with me," she said. Tears welled up in her eyes.

"This isn't for me to see," replied Zero. Dae reluctantly released him and he walked out, closing the heavy steel door behind him. The Hessian waited for him.

"Well?" said The Hessian.

"Well, what? They just got started," replied Zero. "This could take anywhere from a few minutes to a few hours." The Hessian grunted in disapproval.

"While you were in there playing nursemaid to the Blank, we got more intel from Prophet's Grace," he said. He handed Zero a yellowed piece of paper. Zero took it and eyed The Hessian.

"Did you read it?" Zero asked.

"For your eyes only, apparently," replied The Hessian.

"Uh-huh," said Zero, knowing full well that meant the mercenary probably had taken a peek. He looked down at the note.

> DEPARTMENT OF HUMAN ETHICS
> ON FULL ALERT FOR SUBJECT 831.
> SCAVENGER TEAMS SENT TO THE BLAST.
> ZONES 12, 31, AND 84 COMPROMISED.
> PROPHET'S GRACE MOVING TO ZONE 23
> TO RENDEZVOUS WITH SURVIVORS
> FROM ZONE 31. PROTECT SUBJECT 831.

"We have to move, now!" snapped Zero. The Hessian looked at him, puzzled.

"We're going in for an S and R op? I would think that Prophet's Grace could handle picking up a few troops," he said. Zero blew past him and out the door.

"There is no Indigo Group in Zone 31. They are walking right into a trap!"

***

The glass fields of Zone 23 were riddled with the smoking corpses and overturned vehicles. Zero, riding point in his Crawler, looked out and took it all in. They were too late to save anyone. The DHE had already been here and left, leaving nobody from Prophet's Grace alive. The stink of

20

burning corpses filled his nostrils, and the crack of glass underneath the fires echoed through the empty blackness of night.

The Hessian pulled up alongside Zero's Crawler on his bike.

"Scavengers. Armed with at least two B-Tanks. They came to fight," he said, looking out on the aftermath as well.

"They didn't stand a chance," said Zero quietly. He pushed himself out of the hole atop the crawler and jumped off. The ground shattered under the impact of his boots. Black, scorched dust kicked up and Zero pulled his bandanna over his mouth and nose. He walked into the field, examining the bodies. The Hessian turned off his bike and followed.

"Now do you see? This *is* war. The DHE won't ever stop," said The Hessian. He put a hand on Zero's shoulder. Zero stared into the fire blazing about a dead soldier. They had taken his gun and all his B-packs. They didn't want anyone else taking weapons and ammo off these dead men. Indigo Group had just lost over a dozen men, Crawlers, and weapons. This was a hard blow. Then it hit him.

"We have to get back! They are going for Dae!" Zero cried, turning to The Hessian. "Make sure your men are square! We don't know what kind of shit storm we are going home to!" Zero pulled out his Com. "Squad, this is Point. Return to base. We have been compromised and we have Scavengers headed for home. I need every weapon you've got holding a fresh B-pack, every Crawler's bolt thrower warmed up, and every one of you square. They have at least two B-Tanks, and who knows what else. The minute they are in range of the throwers, you let loose!"

The return chatter confirmed his order as Zero mounted his Crawler and started up his bolt thrower. The weapon whirred to life and the barrel cracked with electricity. He heard The Hessian barking orders at his men to split and flank the base. They were going to surround the Scavengers and squeeze. Zero only hoped that the rest of his men inside held out. He hoped Dae was safe.

***

Zero, The Hessian, and their men arrived in time to see the last B-Tank explode. The Com from inside the base was silent, and there was no movement on the outside. What was left of the Scavenger's bodies lay everywhere. Zero dismounted his Crawler and took a closer look. The Scavengers seemed to have been hit with charges, but there was no scorching on their black suits and no blast holes. It was as if their bodies had simply popped.

The Hessian and his men ran to the base's entrance. It was covered in the blood and viscera of the Scavengers. They opened the door, expecting to see their comrades dead, or even a battle still ensuing. There was nothing. All was still. The Hessian motioned to his men to move cautiously, and entered the base. Zero took his gun from its holster and his squad joined them.

Inside, it seemed as if nothing had been touched. All the weapons were in their places and all the Com stations were still on. Zero was confused. It was as if there had been no fighting at all, but the exploded corpses of the Scavengers outside said otherwise.

"Tell your men to stand down," said Zero to The Hessian.

"It could be a trap," said The Hessian, still moving cautiously as if a surprise attack was imminent.

22

"No," said Zero. "Follow me." He headed down a side corridor and towards the room he had left Dae and Vice in. The large steel door was still closed, but from behind it, Zero could hear voices. He approached the door carefully, but the bolt from the inside unlocked and it started to open.

"See, it's just Zero!" said Dae from the other side of the door. Zero motioned for The Hessian to lower his gun.

"Dae?" asked Zero as he entered the room. Inside were all the men and women that had stayed behind while Zero and The Hessian went to help Prophet's Grace. They all stood with shocked looks on their faces, but their eyes weren't on Zero. They were all looking at Dae. The little girl stood in front of Zero and The Hessian, smiling.

"Everybody is fine, Zero. I brought them all here and made the men from the lab go away," she said. Zero looked across the room at Vice. She was visibly shaken. Zero moved past Dae and approached her.

"What happened?" he asked.

"She broke our session half way through. I've never met anyone who could just eject me from their mind," said Vice, still bewildered.

"The Scavengers…Vice, did Dae do that?" Zero asked.

"She brought everyone into the room. No, she *teleported* them into the room. Then we started to hear popping noises. Screams. Explosions," said Vice. "When it stopped, she said you were here. She said the men from the lab were all gone."

"Vice, there are two dozen dead Scavengers outside, and two B-Tanks that look like they've taken heavy fire. Are you telling me—"

"I'm telling you, Dae killed them. She killed them all," said Vice. The fear in her voice was all too apparent. Zero looked over the rest of the soldiers. They all had their eyes still locked on the little girl. Dae stood in the doorway, near The Hessian.

"We're safe now," she said, smiling at Zero. She turned and looked up at The Hessian. "Can we be friends now?" she asked.

The Hessian looked at Zero, and then down at Dae, smiling at the little girl.

"I told him you were a bomb," he said. Dae giggled.

"Boom," she said, and hugged The Hessian's leg.

DEAD RELATIVES

The family Lewis was born into was large. His mother had four sisters and two brothers, each of them with wives or husbands, and children of their own. This made family gatherings quite the circus, and holidays were even more so. When he was young, it was fun to have so many different people and personalities around him. They would laugh and cry, drinking wine and recounting stories that had been told time and time again, but never got old, at least not to Lewis.

The best stories always came from his grandmother on his mother's side. She knew little secrets about everyone in her family and had no qualms about embarrassing anyone with her tails of raising seven children and taking care of the numerous grandchildren that followed. Lewis, being the youngest in the family, aside from a few babies that had been born to his cousins and their significant others, would lose himself in these stories, imagining all of his aunts and uncles as children. In his mind, they were simply shorter versions of their adult selves, and this made the imagery in his head even more hilarious.

The death of Uncle Brian was the first time Lewis had ever dealt with the loss of a family member. At age seven, he didn't know how to process the fact that the man who smoked like a chimney and had the biggest laugh of anybody he knew would never be around again. Instead, he saw Uncle Brian's funeral as just another family gathering. He moved from person to person, telling them all about school and soccer games and all the other stuff children of seven tell their family members. Each one listened and nodded in all the right places, but something was different, Lewis just didn't know what.

25

Next came Lewis's Aunt Michelle. A year after that, the matriarch of the family, his grandmother, passed away as well. The reality of death sank in. Each year after that, Lewis saw the numbers of his large family dwindle. The holidays were no longer filled with laughter, but a somber tone that overtook each of the surviving brothers and sisters.

Each year after, almost like clockwork, another family member would become ill and die. The gatherings ceased all together after a while, and finally, when Lewis was twenty-one, his mother died. The pain of that loss stuck hard with Lewis, but the mechanics of the funeral process had become second nature to him by then. It wasn't that Lewis was cold about losing his mother, quite the opposite in fact. It was that all of the deaths in his family had somehow prepared him for all of it, and instead of being overwhelmed, Lewis mourned silently and in a very personal manner.

Life continued on after that. Lewis had never been especially close to his father until his mother had become ill, and when it had become apparent that they were going to have to be each other's support system through the entire ordeal, the gap began to close. After she passed, Lewis and his father became closer than they had ever been. He moved in with the old man, more out of necessity than obligation, and the two would spend hours at the kitchen table talking about politics, the weather, movies, books, and almost anything they had on their minds. Sometimes the conversation would steer towards the family members who had departed, but never for too long.

At one point, Lewis tried to contact his cousins. It was something he had wanted to do for a while, but there wasn't much of a response on their end. The occasional outing for a beer or a cup of coffee was all he could get out of them, but it was never the same as before. They all had lives of their own and had made their peace with leaving the memories of huge Thanksgiving dinners and towers of presents under Christmas trees behind them. Those days, like the dearly departed, were gone, and they were never coming back. That struck a chord with Lewis harder than losing anyone, even his mother. Not only were the people dead, but any hope of putting the pieces left behind together to make something was dead too. In his mind, Lewis gave up on family, aside from his father. He wouldn't be the only one left to care about such things, and he didn't want to be seen as a nuisance, opening old wounds for his own sense of belonging.

Some months after this revelation, Lewis was once again at the kitchen table with his father. The radio squawked in the background of their conversation over whether or not the Democrats were going to hold the presidency in the fall, of if the Republicans were going to sweep in like a red wave, when the phone rang. Most of the morning callers were either bill collectors or telemarketers, but something made Lewis get up and check the caller ID anyway. To his surprise, it was his Uncle Richie, someone neither he nor his father had heard from in almost three years.

Two things went through Lewis's head in the split-second between hitting the talk button and saying hello. The first was that someone, probably his Aunt Florence, Richie's wife, had died. The second was anger. Anger that it had taken almost three years for Richie or anybody from his mother's family to contact him and his father.

Richie had married into the family, just as Lewis's father had, years before Lewis was born. He had always been a nice enough guy, and had actually encouraged Lewis to go into a scientific field at an early age, possibly one that would bring him to work for Richie one day. The man had made a fortune running a pharmaceutical company that quickly became attached to government and military contracts. Mostly, his company had developed the vaccinations they gave to soldiers when they entered the service, and had even revolutionized a few inoculations against certain agents used in chemical warfare. This brought in even more money.

When Lewis's grandmother had died, Richie and Florence had stepped in to take the reins of the family's affairs until they had degenerated into their current form. Lewis blamed Richie for the disjointed state his family was in, but had made peace with it over the years, knowing that anger only breeds more anger. The last time they had spoken to one another Lewis had been silent throughout the conversation, listening to Richie talk about his company going public with their stock. Lewis feigned interest and then left Richie's enormous house with a bad taste in his mouth.

"Lewis! How have you been?" Richie asked.

"Oh, you know. Same old, same old. How's Florence?" Richie replied.

"Great! Better than great! Lewis, I want you to come up to the cabin this weekend. Bring your dad too. Your cousins are all coming, along with your Uncle Peter and your Aunt Sophia. Everyone will be there."

Lewis couldn't believe what he was hearing. He fell silent and looked over at his father, his eyes wide. The old man looked back at Lewis, puzzled.

"Lewis? Are you there?" Richie asked.

"Y-yeah. I just…what's going on Richie?"

"I have a surprise for everyone. Look, I know it's been a long time kid, but it's time we put our family back together again. I know you've been trying to get in touch with your cousins, and that's why I wanted to make sure they were all coming before I invited you. They all said they would be there. Tell me you'll be there with your dad."

Lewis's head was swimming, but he managed to push out a 'yes'.

"Good to hear! You remember how to get there, right? I'm sure your dad does. Come up Friday night. I have a surprise for the both of you, and I know you'll want to be there for dinner." Richie said. The other end of the line clicked off, and Lewis put the phone down.

Lewis explained what Richie had said to his father, and they both agreed that, while it was out of the blue, it would be good for them to go and see everyone. Lewis's father didn't have much of a family to begin with, and he had always treasured the time he had spent with his wife's family. They had always been good to him and Lewis's grandmother had always been gracious to him. From the old man's perspective, they were good people who had suffered a lot, and now were finally ready to put the past where it belonged.

Lewis was not as optimistic. As he had grown older he saw that Richie always had an angle, no matter the situation. No matter how much he wanted this all to be genuine, there had to be a hitch if Richie was as excited as he sounded on the phone. A chill went up his spine thinking about it.

Friday came and Lewis was packed and ready to go, as was his father. They climbed into the car they shared and made their way towards the highway for the three hour drive in front of them. The excitement on the old man's face was clear, and even his voice perked up more than usual. Lewis swore that if this trip turned into one of Richie's schemes and he had gotten his father's hopes up for nothing, he would punch the man's lights out. Screwing with *his* mind was one thing, but getting his father's hopes up only to dash them was something different altogether.

The drive up was filled with classic rock and old stories about going fishing with Lewis's uncles at the same cabin they were headed to. Lewis had heard all of these stories before, but they hadn't been told in so long that he honestly didn't mind. It took the edge off all of his misgivings and instilled just a bit of excitement in him to see the people he had given up on, even Richie.

Lewis and his father pulled on to a back road some hours later and approached the cabin shortly thereafter. Cars lined the driveway, and Lewis figured they were the last to arrive. Hearing the rumble of their engine, Richie came out to the front porch of the cabin and waved. Lewis put the car in park and got out, his father doing the same. The two moved to the trunk to unload their bags as Richie came running up to them. Lewis was surprised that the man had lost weight over the years and his hair was played with more grey than it had been. He looked older, but wore it well.

"Don't worry about the bags right now guys. There will be time for that. Everyone is in the living room and are waiting to see you," he said. Lewis's father put his hand out to Richie with a smile. Richie shook it and pulled him in for a hug.

"It's been a while, Rich," his father said.

"That it has, Tom. Hope you're ready for this," replied Richie. Again, a shiver went up Lewis's spine. "I've been putting this together for almost three years now. And I know you of all people will appreciate it."

"Three years? Didn't think it would be that hard to get everyone together at the same time, but I guess everyone is pretty busy nowadays."

Richie smiled even bigger than before and looked over at Lewis.

"How've you been kid?" he asked. Lewis held back the urge to just outright ask him what the angle was.

"Fine. Still working. Still taking care of this old codger," he said. Richie laughed.

"Good to know. Now come on in guys. Let's not keep everyone waiting any longer."

Richie led the way with the old man behind him and Lewis taking up the rear. The old stairs to the cabin groaned under their feet and the screen door on the front creaked the same way it always had. Memories of summers spent up at the cabin seeped out of the corners of Lewis's mind from the sounds, but it was the smell that brought him back to that time long passed. The cabin always had the smell of sawdust and old bonfires attached to it, and it hadn't changed a bit. To the right of the entrance was the pantry and to the left was the living room. Right in front was the staircase that led to the four bedrooms where the adults had slept while the kids camped out in the backyard, halfway between the cabin and the lake. Many a ghost story had been told in those tents out back, and there had been nights where Lewis had only fallen asleep out of sheer exhaustion, not wanting to close his eyes because of the horrible things that could be lurking in the darkness just out of sight.

Richie and Lewis's father walked into the living room where everyone was gathered. Lewis followed and looked around seeing faces he hadn't seen in years. His cousins, fourteen of them in all were greeting his father. They made their way to him and he was caught in a sea of 'good to see you' and hugs. A few of the children ran around in the crowd, and Lewis struggled to remember their names after not seeing them for so long. At the back of the room, Lewis could make out his Uncle Peter and Aunt Sophia talking to someone. Peter was holding his grandchild that Lewis

31

thought was named Christian, but again couldn't remember. The little boy whined to get down and Peter bent down, letting him run off. Lewis got a good look at the person Peter and Sophia were talking to. It was his Uncle Brian.

Lewis's knees went weak. His eyes opened wide and he pointed to Uncle Brian from across the room. The large man, cigarette hanging out of his mouth just as it had when Lewis was just a young boy, looked back and waved. Uncle Peter and Aunt Sophia looked over at Lewis and smiled. Lewis suddenly realized that everyone was looking at him. The room fell silent. A hand came down on his shoulder and he turned.

"Hello Lewis," said a voice. Lewis turned to see Aunt Michelle standing next to him. He jerked away and bumped into one of his cousins who steadied him.

"No..." he whispered. Lewis turned towards his father who wore an expression of shock that mimicked his own. Tears filled the old man's eyes.

"I think I owe you a bit of an explanation kid," said Richie.

"W-what did you do Richie?" Lewis stammered.

"Well, it was a long process, but this started out as something I was working on for the military. They wanted the ability to reanimate soldiers. You don't have to worry about soldiers dying in the field if they are already dead. The thing is, I saw it as something different kid. I saw it as a way to take away all the despair this family has gone through over the years. I saw it as a chance to bring us all together again. Now, it took a lot of money and some doing, but I managed to get ahold of all of their bodies without anyone being tipped off. Nobody but the family knows they're here and I've had the scientists who worked on them...taken care of."

That was the angle Lewis had been looking for in Richie's invitation. All of the dead relatives, all of the loved ones lost over the years, were here again. Everything became distant to Lewis, as if he were in a dream. His father began to cry.

"No. You bastard, no! How could you do this?!" cried the old man. The atmosphere of the room shifted. The expressions on everyone's faces turned sour.

"Tom, Lewis, you have to be able to see what a miracle this is! Of course, they will never be able to leave here in case somebody saw them, but we can all come here whenever we want! I've stocked the place with everything we could need! And they don't need to eat or drink at all! They're happy. We're happy. Can't you see what I've done for you? For all of us?" Richie said.

"Hey Tom. How's it hangin?" called Uncle Brian from the back of the room. Lewis's father pointed a finger at the dead man.

"You aren't Brian! Brain is dead! This is wrong, and you are some kind of abomination! Something...something unnatural!" he yelled. The old man turned to Richie, his face red and tears streaming down his cheeks. "Rich...you didn't...she's not...Clarice isn't..." the old man sobbed.

"She's out back with her mother, Tom," said Richie. Hearing this, Lewis snapped back. A sense of rage overtook him at what Richie had done. He stepped up to the man and threw a right hook, knocking Richie to the floor. His cousins sprang to life grabbing his arms.

"You bastard!" he cried as his cousins restrained him.

"Let go of my son!" his father yelled. The old man grabbed Lewis's shirt collar and pulled him from the fray. "We're leaving! Don't ever try to contact us again. Monsters, all of you!" Lewis and his father turned to leave.

33

"Lewis...Tom..." said a voice from behind them. They both paused knowing full well who it belonged to.

"Oh god," said Lewis. He could feel the tears coming. He turned and looked at his father. The old man sighed heavily and hung his head. It was Clarice, Lewis's mother.

"You aren't my wife. My wife died three years ago," he said and walked out of the door.

"Lewis...please," said the voice. Lewis didn't turn around. He didn't want to see her standing there. If he had, he might have lost the sense of just how horrible the thing Richie had done really was. More than anything, Lewis had wanted to have a family again, but not like this. He followed his father outside.

They got to their car and Lewis climbed in the driver's seat. His father had his head in his hands as he cried loudly.

"Drive son. Get us the hell out of here."

After that, not a word passed between them the entire way home.

In the years that passed, neither of them ever spoke about what had happened at the cabin, and they were never contacted by any family members again. Lewis married later in life and had a beautiful daughter not long after. His father survived long enough to play with his grandchild, but died when she turned seven. Besides the old man's work buddies from long ago, the only people at his funeral were Lewis, his wife, and their daughter. His family. His only family. That was enough for Lewis, and he never wished for anything more.

GAME

"We were fighting the Hellspawned Knight, and Christopher was falling asleep at the table," said Dan, reminding the rest of his party where they had left off at the previous game session.

"I wasn't falling asleep, I was just figuring out what to do on my next turn," said Christopher.

"Yeah, you were completely conscious when you pitched forward and bounced your head off the table," exclaimed Ryan. Everyone except Christopher laughed.

"Just make sure his caffeine intake is doubled this week. I'm tired of cutting sessions short lately, and I want this fight over with," said Thomas. He looked at his four friends sitting around the table and, in his head, laughed. He knew that once his Hellspawned Knight unleashed its special ability, the whole game was going to be turned on its head. Thomas wasn't going to kill them, no, that would be tantamount to cheating. The fate he had in store for his players was much more devious, and it was almost time to let his plan unfold.

Coming up with such a diabolical plan hadn't taken long, and Thomas had based the entire game he ran around it. He had already intended to get his friends together for a Fantastic Planes game, but for a role-playing game such as this, you needed a story, and it had to be epic. And, as everyone knows, every epic story needs an epic villain. This was where the Hellspawned Knight came into play. It would not only be the bad guy, but the story as well.

The idea was that the Knight would have the ability to move between all of the Fantastic Planes at will, which would make him very powerful and very dangerous. The plot, however, was to move the whole party to a randomized plane and make them fight the Knight somewhere alien to them. Throwing them off their game and possibly stranding them on an alien world would have them shaken by the end of the night. It was the perfect plan, and it's time had come.

"I need Toshi's sheet. Anyone see it?" asked Jason. Thomas looked through his stack of papers and found Jason's character. Jason was the newest player, so he wasn't that proficient in the game system, but he had some very good ideas throughout their sessions, and his character, a samurai with a haunted sword, was shaping up to be quite the bad-ass. Thomas handed Jason the character and moved on to the rest.

Next handed out was Christopher's cyborg-cowboy with the gun arm. It was a monster of a character on the battlefield, but having only one arm made him almost useless for much else. Thomas then handed Ryan his magic-wielding vampire. It was the most bastardized thing Thomas had ever seen, and he knew that Ryan was cheating on his rolls to make it hit succeed on everything it did. Finally, Thomas gave the gargoyle with a knack for alchemy to Dan. It had been the closest thing to a healer in the group so far, but Dan only used it in such a capacity when someone was only a round or two from having to make a new character from scratch. Separate, the characters were almost unplayable, but together, they made a formidable party that had defied every monster, trap, or plot hook Thomas had thrown at them. Every single one except the Hellspawned Knight.

"Everyone set?" asked Thomas. The players answered with a resounding yes. "Great, then roll initiative."

Everyone, including Thomas, rolled their dice. Thomas didn't need to roll, but he did anyways just to make the players more comfortable. He had already decided that the Hellspawned Knight would go last, giving each player a chance to see how useless their characters were against such a powerful enemy. Writing down the numbers that the players had rolled, Thomas determined that it would be Jason acting first, then Dan, followed by Ryan and Christopher.

"Jason, you're up." Thomas said. Jason looked at the map in front of him. There were four small figurines placed on it representing the characters, and one over-sized army man that represented the Hellspawned Knight. After a moment, Jason looked up at Thomas.

"I'm going to rush in and full on attack this guy with my blade," he said. Thomas held back a laugh.

"Go right ahead," said Thomas. "Make your rolls." Jason rolled a few dice, and Thomas could see he was trying to do the math in his head. After a moment, Jason's face lit up and he looked over at Thomas.

"Twenty-nine to hit," Jason said, triumphantly. Thomas didn't even have to look at the stats of his Hellspawned Knight to know that wasn't going to be enough to hit.

"Nope. Sorry. Dan, you're up," said Thomas. The look on Jason's face went from satisfaction to confusion. Dan picked up his dice and rolled.

"Thirty-two on a ranged attack with a bottle of liquid fire," Dan said with a hint of arrogance in his voice. Thomas was starting to enjoy dashing his player's pride.

"Sorry, man. No go," said Thomas.

"I call bullshit! That was almost the best I can do without a critical hit!" said Dan.

"Well, do better next time," said Thomas, smiling at Dan. It was almost too bad that Dan wouldn't get another roll. Satisfaction set in. Thomas was proud of his big baddie, and the fight was going exactly as planned.

"I suppose it'd going to be up to me to save all of your asses, isn't it?" said Ryan. "I'm going to move to the Knight and try a bite attack."

"You're seriously going to try a bite attack on that thing?!" yelled Dan.

"I can do what I want!" scolded Ryan. He rolled. "Perfect twenty!" Thomas knew he hadn't rolled a perfect twenty. Any time Ryan rolled an "incredible score" he scooped his die up right away, like he did after the bite attack at that moment. Fortunately, Thomas had built his Knight out of stronger stuff than that.

"Doesn't matter. What did you get for a full score?" asked Thomas. Ryan shot him a glance as if he had just been slapped. Anger and confusion showed all over his face, and Thomas just looked back at him, waiting for the answer.

"Twenty-nine," said Ryan.

"Sorry, man," said Thomas.

"That's really dumb! I can't even hit it if I roll a perfect twenty?!" cried Ryan. Thomas knew this was going to happen. He had to act quickly or the night would degenerate into an argument instead of any actual gaming.

"Christopher, you're up," said Thomas. This was the only character in the group that Thomas was honestly wary of. The cyborg-cowboy had the potential to do real damage to the Hellspawned Knight. Without hesitation, Christopher rolled his attack.

"Thirty-six," said Christopher. He had managed to hit it. Thomas had jacked up the Knight's hit points, so there wasn't much to worry about from just one attack. It was the two other attacks that were quick to follow that he was worried about.

"Thirty-four on the second, and thirty-four on the third as well," said Christopher. All three were hits. Thomas held his breath as Christopher rolled damage for each of them. "Forty-two," he said.

Thomas breathed a sigh of relief. Christopher hadn't done in the Knight. He had been saved by piss poor dice rolls. It was time for the Knight to act, and not a moment too soon.

"Okay, you four see this swirling light between yourselves and the Hellspawned Knight," said Thomas. Ryan spoke up immediately.

"I'm going to do a Magic Knowledge check," Ryan started.

"On your turn," replied Thomas, cutting Ryan off before he could roll out of turn. The anger coming off of Ryan was almost palpable, but Thomas knew it wouldn't last. He started again. "As I was saying, you see a swirling light that opens up, and you see another world on the other side."

"Oh no, please say you're not doing what I think you're doing," said Dan. Dan had played with Thomas before, and knew that he had a thing for plane jumping. It was just one of those neat little skills Thomas found himself attracted to.

"What's he doing?" asked Jason.

"We're going to a different plane, aren't we, Thomas?" asked Dan. The party groaned in displeasure, but Thomas didn't care. This was *his* game.

"Yep, and you feel the vortex sucking you in. Everyone make a resistance check." Each person made their rolls and, as predicted, each person lost. It was time for Thomas to work his magic. As the guy running the game, it fell on Thomas to roll the plane they were to travel to. He opened the large book containing the rules and began rolling dice.

"This always takes forever," said Dan. Thomas looked up from the large tome with a hard stare.

"I know what I'm doing," he said, looking right at Dan. Dan put his hands up, signaling he would back down, and Thomas went back to rolling. A few moments and some scribbled notes later, Thomas looked across at his party. This was going to burn them pretty hard, but it would be worth it.

"Okay, first you see five people on the other side. They look to be humans. It's a mundane world, so you can feel the lack of magic," said Thomas, pointing to Ryan.

"Son of a bitch," muttered Ryan. This just made Thomas smile. It hadn't been his plan to send them to a mundane world, but that's what he had rolled on the random plane generator. Ryan's character would be almost useless, except for the fact that he was a vampire.

"Can they see us yet?" asked Dan.

"Not until you cross the barrier," replied Thomas. Dan looked around at Jason, Ryan, and Christopher. He was smiling ear to ear, and Thomas felt uneasy. He had an idea and was certain to get the rest to follow him.

"Everyone, relent on the last Resistance check and hold until my action," said Dan.

"Why would we do that?!" cried Ryan. Jason and Christopher, also looking puzzled, waited for an answer.

"We are all pretty close to leveling, right?" asked Dan. The group nodded in agreement. Thomas didn't like what he was hearing. "Then all we have to do is relent, get sucked over to a new plane, attack and kill the humans, and we will level up. Then we can try and find a way to get back later."

"I hate to say it, but that sounds like the best plan we have," said Ryan.

"What about the knight?" Christopher asked.

"Worse comes to worse, he can try and follow us, but he will have no magic either. He will have to chase us to get

40

to us. And since most of us are pretty good when it comes to straight combat, it could even out the fight," explained Dan.

"I'm in," said Jason. Christopher agreed with the other three as well. Thomas scowled. They had managed to find a way to level the playing field, with the help of his random plane generator. He couldn't just go back and change where they were going. He had committed them to one place, and he wasn't going to freak out because it wasn't going as he had planned. Thomas knew that even the best plots come undone from time to time in a game like Fantastic Planes, so he did what he thought was best. He let them proceed with their plan.

"Then it's settled. We are going to hold our actions until we cross into the other plane," said Dan. He smiled triumphantly at Thomas, and it took everything Thomas had to not reach out and slap him.

"Make your resistance checks," said Thomas. One by one, each player relented. Thomas sighed. Just then, the wall behind him exploded and Thomas sprawled forward on the table.

Before any of them could react, the strangers were on them. Jason never had a chance to move before the one with the sword took his head off with one swift blow. Dan screamed and tried to run, but another one of the strangers was on him. Dan's scream intensified as the winged thing threw some kind of acid on him. His skin began to sizzle and melt, revealing bone underneath. Ryan jumped up and ran at the thing throwing acid on Dan. He leapt forward to tackle it, but was intercepted by a black shadow.

"Thought you could take on my gargoyle friend, eh, mortal?" asked the stranger. Ryan looked at his attacker. He was pale with jet black hair and eyes to match. And he had fangs.

41

"No," he whispered.

"Yes," said the vampire. He bit deeply into Ryan's neck.

Christopher was terrified. He rose slowly, hoping he wouldn't attract the attention of the things that had attacked his friends. He heard a click behind him.

"Nothing personal, son. Wrong place, wrong time," said a voice. Before Christopher could turn around, a gunshot went off and his brains were splattered all over the wall.

The gunshot roused Thomas. The explosion had stunned him and he had been on the verge of unconsciousness, but he was awake now. As the carnage came into view, Thomas' eyes widened. It couldn't be them. It was a game, that's all. Just a game.

"It's here! Run!" yelled the cyborg cowboy. All of the characters looked up at Thomas in wide-eyed horror. They were afraid of him? A hand landed on his shoulder. It wasn't him they were staring at. It was whoever was standing *behind* him. It could only be…

"You have done well my friend, but your usefulness has run its course," said the person behind Thomas in a dark and booming voice. He didn't have to turn around to know who it was.

"But, it's just a game," said Thomas. It was the last thing he ever did before the Hellspawned Knight brought his sword down on his neck.

DUST

It was the Dust. It was always the Dust. I wouldn't even be here if it weren't for the blasted stuff. If Pete would have told me what I was getting into before we left my home, I wouldn't have even come. At times I wonder if this whole mess would have gotten back to the place I came from had things gone differently, but they didn't and for that I am truly grateful. It's funny. I can't even remember what my home was called now. I've been here so long that my first clear memory of anything is being here. It's what happens to anyone who has been here a long time, but the Dust speeds the process up. Eventually, the past doesn't matter. It's the future that matters. The future, and the next time you can get the Dust.

I can't remember the name of the boy that told me Pete used to be a real "stand up bloke" but I remember what he looked like; short, stubby little kid that always wore clothes that were too small for him. He was younger than me by far, but he knew more about being on the island than anyone else. I really wish I remembered his name. He was the first one to die when Pete went crazy. He deserves more of a memory than "the little fat kid" but I can't give him that. Not anymore.

As near as I can gather the war was sparked off when the native girl killed one of the little bug-things that lived on the island. That thing, screaming there in the dark, was the first casualty. He was pretty low by that point, so madness was just a small push away. It's hazy, but I know it was something the native girl said or did that gave him that push.

Her name is lost to me as well, but I would curse it if I could remember what it was. She's the one who got Pete started on the Dust long before I got here, and she was the

43

one who ended up giving it to the people on the beach as well. If there was a single person that could be held responsible for everything that happened after I showed up, it would be her. But she's dead now and that is the only thing I would deem to be punishment enough for everything she incited.

I can only assume I flew to the island like the rest of us had done. I don't remember it, but that's how it went; Pete would fly out, pick up a few new recruits, get them hooked on the Dust, and they would follow him and his promises of more back to the island. Because that's what happens, you see. You try it that first time and you think it's the greatest feeling in the world. You're truly free. Nothing else matters, and you are invincible. Nothing can touch you. The stuff is courage and happiness and love, all rolled into one. And then you want it again. I don't remember my first time any longer, and that's a small miracle. I've been off of the stuff for a long time, but I still crave it, and the memory of that first thrill with it would just bring back that pang of desire in my chest again.

Let me piece together what I *do* remember. The natives lived on the other side of the forest from us, and somewhere to the north was where the bug-things had their colony. That was where the Dust came from; it came off of the bug-things. The natives would use it for their rituals, but it was that damned girl who brought one of the bug-things to Pete. That's what the little fat kid told me. It was some kind of pet that he kept, and it didn't even need to be caged. The bug just stayed by him, sitting on his shoulder or buzzing about his head, and always giving off dust. Some days, he would be virtually covered in the stuff.

The little fat kid told me a lot about the other guys on the boat too, but that doesn't matter. Pete killed them all. *We* killed them all.

I remember snorting the Dust. That was just how you did it; a quick bump off of the back of your hand. Then one of the new guys Pete brought showed us how to "cook" it. We put it over a fire in small batches and watched the color go from a brilliant gold to a black that was darker than the night sky. Then we would take thin, hollow reed and sharpen them to points sucking up the black sludge into them. You could poke it into your arm with ease, and the sludge would slide right into you. Even if I don't remember my own name, I will always remember the feeling of that stuff pumping into my blood that first time. What I told you about Dust before, imagine that but more of it and much quicker. We weren't just boys when we were shooting it up. It made us gods.

I remember being told that there was a time of balance on the island, but then someone pissed off the bug-things. I don't remember who did it, but I can only assume it was one of us. The other guys never came off of their beach, and the natives had too much respect for the creatures. They began attacking people that came near their nest or colony or whatever bug-things have. That meant us, the natives, and the other guys. The one Pete kept as a pet would scream in the night, keeping us all awake. I remember that the girl killed it. The next morning we found it stuck to a tree, flayed open and its wings torn off. Pete gave us a speech about respect and loyalty. It was inspiring. The girl stood next to him, giggling and clapping when he said that we were going to turn against the natives who had so obviously pissed off the bug-things and take their Dust supply. We couldn't get any more and it we had become desperate. The little golden flecks that had grown over the holes we put in ourselves

45

with reeds ached. Our brains felt two sizes too big for our heads. A few of us couldn't sleep anymore from the pain. Pete had brought us here to be peacekeepers, but with the Dust, that all changed. Now, without it, we were all feeling like scared little children.

Some of us died in the raid on the natives' camp, but we won in the end. They never saw it coming. They thought of us as friends. We came in the night and killed half of them before the other half knew what was going on. We took their Dust supply. We killed women and children. The girl cackled like she was possessed as the camp burned. Pete dragged their chief out and cut his head off with that piece of twisted steel he always had at his side. By the time the dawn came, we were back at our camp celebrating and pumping Dust into our veins. Everything after that is clear to me.

By the morning, we were out of Dust again, so Pete went to go get more from the bug-things. Now, why he thought he could do it when they wouldn't let the natives close and he had slaughtered the one he kept as a pet is beyond my recognition *now*, but it wasn't then. Actually, I remember thinking that it was an absolutely brilliant idea. But after a while the girl said she was going out to look for him. When Pete came back empty handed and covered in scratches, we knew we had a problem.

We told Pete the girl had gone looking for him and he freaked out. He yelled and screamed and licked whatever bloody reeds he could find, hoping for just a speck or two to calm the aches. He didn't find anything and we all sat there watching and waiting for orders.

We organized into search parties as best we could to head into the forest, but the lack of sleep and Dust was starting to get to everyone. We must have been out there for a few hours before we heard someone call out that they had

46

spotted her. It was the little fat kid. He started to tell some of us what he had seen, but we shut him up right away. That was one of the rules; if you learn something new, you tell Pete first. If it was worth knowing, Pete *had* to know it first.

Pete showed shortly after and the kid told him he had seen the girl walking up from the beach. The thing was, she was walking away from where the other guys had docked their boat, and it looked like she had Dust with her.

Pete gave the kid the long stare he was so good at giving. It seemed to say "do you think I'm an idiot" and made anyone on the receiving end feel very small. But the kid, half out of it and needing Dust so bad that he was stumbling on his own words, kept it up. He asked Pete why his girl would even be talking to the other guys. He asked why she had Dust when everyone knew the other guys weren't supposed to have it at all. He asked and asked. Pete moved quicker than I had ever seen him move before. A splash of blood and a flash of twisted steel, and the little fat kid had been relieved of the head that had dared imply that Pete's girl had been consorting with the enemy.

Nobody moved. Even if we had, what were we going to do? Pete could have killed all of us in the blink of an eye. Standing there, covered in blood, I almost thought he would. Those few moments seemed to drag on for hours, until the girl showed up. Pete dropped his steel and ran to her. They threw their arms around each other and just stood there. We all walked back to our camp, leaving the two of them behind along with the kid's body.

That night, we could hear the girl's cries of pleasure coming from the forest.

The next morning, Pete told us all how the girl had bravely allowed herself to be captured by the enemy, only to escape with a good amount of their treasure and their Dust.

47

We were all stunned, yet overjoyed. This time, Pete said, we would ration out what we had so that it would keep us going for longer. He then revealed his plan to go back into the forest and begin capturing the bug-things to harvest them for Dust. Since they wouldn't give it to us willingly, we would take it by force. This was no longer a choice for anyone. It was the strongest imposing their dominance on the weaker inhabitants of the island. There would be order, and it would be Pete's order.

The battles that happened after seem like one big battle to me now. Sometimes it would be the bug-things and us. Other times it would be the bug-things fighting off the other guys, but we would sneak in from behind and capture as many of them as we could. We used to fight the other guys openly, but now we just stayed out of each other's way. We seemed to have the same goals in getting what Dust we could, and Pete said that he was sure their leader probably knew, as he did, that it would be us and them at the end. When all the bug-things were dead or captured, we would fight again. Years later, that's exactly what happened.

Pete woke us one night; he was naked and screaming that he had come up with the final solution to the whole thing. It was draining our resources for him to leave the island and bring back new recruits, and the bug-things had gotten adept at killing us. They were organized in swarms like we had never seen. Even the other guys felt the shift as their raids became fewer and fewer, at least from what intelligence we could gather. The only solution was to scorch the land. If we burned down the forest, there would be no place for them to hide. Whichever ones didn't die would join the ones we had captured in cages.

We planned it out meticulously. We started with the edges and fanned the flames inwards, making escape impossible unless the things went straight up. That's when we would let loose. The fire raged, and like a shining tornado, they poured upwards. Arrows flew from the war machines we had built. For a moment, the shining sun was blotted out by their numbers. Their screams echoed over the whole island. Pete cleaned up any that evaded our attacks. He seemed to delight in being covered in blood and Dust high above the treetops. I know now that by that point he had gone completely mad. Any trace of the Pete we knew was gone. All that was left in his life was war and Dust.

The other guys didn't bother us. They just sat and watched from the beaches. They watched us commit genocide. I wonder now if they knew that the tide of war was headed their way at that moment. Their leader had always been a bright fellow, and on more than a few occasions he had gone blow for blow with Pete, so it is safe to assume that when he looked out and saw that the forest was a raging inferno, he knew.

It was almost another year when the truth about the girl's relationship with the men on the beach was revealed. Pete had become quite paranoid by then. To pull someone out of a war so suddenly doesn't get rid of the instincts and impulses that come from it. Those lingered, and soon festered within Pete. He was suspicious of everyone on good days. Others, he wouldn't come out into the open for enormous lengths of time. The girl always came and went though.

It was after one of his long stays indoors that he found her on the beach. She had left hours earlier, and apparently had not returned quick enough for Pete's taste. He came out and we all greeted him, but he walked past us as if he didn't hear us at all. At the edge of the camp, he took off running through the blackened forest. We all went on high alert, trusting that Pete knew what he was doing and that if he was panicked, we should all be panicked. Around an hour later he came covered in blood with tears running down his face. In one hand, he held his sword. In the other, he held the girl's head.

He told us that he had seen her come from the beach when the little fat kid's voiced echoed in his head. The questions from years earlier resurfaced. Peter waited, and when he was sure that she had not been followed, he ambushed her.

Pete told us the confession she had cried as he cut her. She had been lying with the leader of the other guys since the beginning. Every time she went to him, she went willingly, and she brought Dust with her. In fact, she had brought them some of the captured bug-things. And then, he told us of how she had laughed at him. He didn't tell us what she had said exactly that incurred his final blow, but we could all see how horribly it had scarred him. He cried, and we cried with him. We cried for him. That night, we ran the Dust supplies low.

He didn't wait. If we would have planned the battle as we had with the bug-things, I may not be the last person alive on the island, but off we went to war the next day. They blew some of us away with the cannons on their ship. The rest of us boarded them and found our enemies well matched. For every one of them that went down, one of us fell as well.

Amidst the battle, Pete and their leader fought. Before, they were an even match. Now, with the Dust coursing through his veins, the leader had the upper hand. He was bigger and stronger than Pete, and always had been, but the Dust had tipped the scales just slightly in Pete's favor. Now, Pete was forced backwards with the power of the man's

50

attacks. They were both possessed by something, and at one point I wondered if that battle would simply go on forever.

Finally, as he disarmed Pete, the man swung his other hand and buried an oversized hook deep in Pete's skull. I remember the sight of it; the look of shock on his face and the blood that came out the corners of his eyes. Something inside me snapped. I pulled a pistol from one of the others corpses and blew the leader's head off. Then, I blacked out.

When I awoke on the deck of the ship, fire was everywhere. Instinct took over and I ran to the edge of the boat, jumping overboard. I swam for my life even though everything in my body screamed in pain. When I reached the sand, I laid there for hours. Bodies of my friends washed ashore, along with those of our enemies. Eventually I stood and made my way back to our camp, leaving the corpses to the sun and sand.

It took me days to process what had happened. I held out hope that someone would come along. Friend or foe, I couldn't be the last one left alive. I just couldn't. But the coldness of reality crept in and I realized that I was really, truly alone. I did nothing but cry for a few days after that.

After dealing with the bodies of everyone I found, I set about killing the bug-things. As I said, those that hadn't been burned in the fire were in cages, so it was easy. I felt no remorse as I did it. If they were still there, anyone who came to the island could be seduced by the Dust, and the whole thing would start over again. I couldn't let that happen. They chirped in terror as I killed each of them. What Dust we had stockpiled I took to the highest ridge overlooking the sea and dumped it. It formed a beautiful golden cloud as the wind took it. By then, I was thinking clearly for the first time in what I can only assume had been decades.

Now, the forest has grown back. The camp is long gone, but I have built myself a fine place. I hunt what animals are left and I fish. I grow green things in the garden I have built. By my count, it has been two centuries since the last battle, and I have not seen a single person since. I guess if Pete didn't bring them here, nobody came to the island. Even if I had the Dust to get me somewhere else, I don't think I would ever bring anyone back with me. This used to be a place of imagination and wonder, but to me it is still a place of horror and war and I am its last protector, damned to spend eternity here alone. The last one alive.

But now you are here too, and I'm not sure how you got here, but I can only assume that somewhere along the way to wherever it was you were going, you got lost. That's how I used to feel. That's how we all used to feel. Just a bunch of lost boys in a land you've never heard of.

LOVE OF DEATH

It's better if I speak to you like this, that way you will only listen and not scream. I would love nothing more than to hear your voice, but I know I wouldn't be able to say what I have to say if you had the chance to interrupt me or ask questions. Here and now, I can speak the truth, undeterred.

I long for you, and I can't express how hard it is for me to say that. In fact, I have never said that to anyone before. For as long as I have been watching over you I have had this feeling that there was something different about you than every other person I have met. There is something so much more vibrant in your eyes, and I feel if you were to look upon me, I would be blinded by your light. It is truly something to behold.

There is no way for us to be together, and after pondering this for a time, I know that to be the truest thing I have ever spoken. Not now. In fact, I'm certain that nobody would ever be able to love me in the way I love you. After everything I have done over the years, no matter how necessary it is, nobody could look upon me with love in their eyes. There are some that believe they yearn for me, but when I come, they are as frightened children. I don't blame them. My visage is a terrifying sight. It is a reminder that sometimes the thing you think you want so badly can turn out to be the thing that brings you the most sadness. Life can be a series of half-hearted choices, but I am an absolute, and a painful one at that.

I know you have contempt for me, what with the pain I have caused you over the years. I have heard your curses, and they have done just that – cursed me. I apologize for every tear you have shed in my wake. There's another thing I have never done. Apologies are not in my nature. What I do,

I do because it is needed, but more than that, it is simply the way of things. But you are the only person I have ever felt sorrow for. I have watched you weep countless tears, and I cannot express how horrible it has made me feel. I wish I could have comforted you, but it was never the right time.

If there was a way I could show you how I adore you, I would, but I know there is not. And I can only hope that when you wake up, you remember that out of all the people in the world, you are the one I hold above the rest. All that have come and gone, and all that will be. One day we will meet, and you will look upon me with the terror all others have, but instead of my cold touch, I will embrace you and wipe away your tears. Until that day, remember that I, Death, am always watching over you.

Sweet dreams.

Zombie Love Slave

You don't forget your first true love. Ever. It's a kind of curse. You could ask a hundred people, and each one would probably say they have had a true love in their life, but only six or seven of them would really mean it. I know this because I would have been one of the other ninety-four or so until I met Alice.

It's better if I skip the beginning of how we met because you know it already. We were a classic case of head-over-heels in love with each other from the get go, and I'm almost certain it made our friends sick to see us always holding hands, kissing, and doing all the things new couples do. We didn't want to spend a moment apart, but life has a way of getting in the way of…well…your life. Sometimes fate, if such a thing exists, decides to give you something beautiful, only to take it away. And although this seems cruel, there is nothing you can do about it no matter how many tears you shed or how many times you plead with the intangible.

We were happy, but that happiness was taken away in a cruel twist of fate one morning. I woke up with Alice lying next to me, her long black hair tickling my face. I put my arm around her to pull her close, and she was cold. But not like the cold you get from sleeping without a blanket on a winter's night. She was as cold as the grave. I pulled more blankets on top of her and held her close, but something was wrong. It hit me seconds later that she wasn't breathing. Alice, with her soft pale skin and big brown eyes that would glitter when the moonlight hit them just right, was dead. And that was just the start of my problems.

I didn't panic. The thought to get up and call 911 was there, but I was too numb to act on it. I rolled her over and looked at her. Her eyes were open, and that was when I broke. They stared at nothing in particular, and I understood right there what life itself was because I couldn't see it within her any longer. Deep sobs escaped me but sounded far off in my own mind, as if they weren't coming from me. I don't know how long I sat there crying over her body, but when I finally regained some semblance of composure, I knew that I had to call the police immediately.

I backed up off of the foot of the bed we had shared, not taking my eyes off of Alice. I reached for my pants and pulled my phone from the pocket. I unlocked it and went to dial 911.

"What are you doing?"

I jumped and dropped the phone. In the split second I had looked away, Alice had sat up and was staring at me with her lifeless eyes, her head cocked to the side just slightly and an inquisitive look on her face. I reached for the words, but didn't have them. I opened my mouth to try and force a response, but I screamed instead. Alice started to laugh, which was really not the response I expected. My scream trailed off into a low squeak, but there I stood, naked and my face twisted into an expression of horror.

"You scream like a little girl," she said. "Now are you done?"

"I...you...you're,"

"Yes Neil, I'm dead. Now get back into bed. It's our day off, and I do not want to spend it trying to coax you down from the ceiling."

Why I did as she asked, I'll never know, but I crawled back into bed and laid down flat on my back, staring at the ceiling. She wrapped herself around me, pressing her cold skin against mine. Time seemed to drag on forever as I stared at the ceiling, hoping to wake up from whatever nightmare I was in. But instead, it got worse.

"I'm totally in the mood," she said. I said nothing. She reached under the sheets and started to touch me. Then, she moved all the way under the sheets and started to use her cold, dry tongue. Fear gripped me and any thoughts of jumping up and running from the bedroom were gone. I couldn't move despite how much I wanted to. "Am I doing something wrong?" she asked from under the sheets. She threw them back and looked at me. "You're not even hard."

I still couldn't speak, and if I was in shock, it had set in by then. The look of hurt in Alice's dead eyes was enough to drive me insane. My dead girlfriend was sad that I couldn't get it up for her, and I was paralyzed with fear. My heart was about to leap from my body. I looked down my chest at her and knew she was expecting a response.

"It's not you. I just…uh…"

"Is it because I'm dead?" she asked. One thing I had learned about Alice over the time we had been together was that almost every question she asked like that, leaving out the "dead" part, was loaded. I don't know why I answered her, but I did.

"Yes. I mean, it's not…" I didn't get the rest out before she threw the cover back over her head and squeezed my balls until I thought they were going to burst. I let out a painful whimper, but was still too scared to do much of anything besides lay there. Questions of whether or not I was doomed to be killed by my zombie girlfriend for not getting a hard-on raced through my head. Every answer I found was "probably". So, I did what anyone would have done in that situation. I fantasized.

I imagined she was alive again. I imagined that she had woken up as perky as ever and had reached over for me. I

57

imagined her naked breasts bouncing as she climbed on top of me and took me inside of her. I could almost feel her rocking back and forth, stuttering as she breathed and letting out little moans of pleasure. She ran her hands along my chest, pushing herself back and forth along the length of me. I put my left hand on her hip, guiding her, while my right hand ran between her breasts and up to her mouth. She lightly sucked on my finger and I could feel her hot breath as she cried out. Then, in a moment of ecstasy, we came together. She collapsed on my chest and we both laid there breathing heavily, our bodies humming with electricity.

I opened my eyes and felt the cold, dead body lying on top of me.

"I love it when you come inside me," she said. Again, I was frozen; half from the orgasm and half from mortal terror. She rolled off of me and lay down on her side of the bed, facing away from me.

I don't know how long I laid there before I got up again, but this time Alice didn't disturb me. I got to my phone and called the police. They arrived shortly after with a paramedic. When they got to the door, I told them I had woken up and there had been something seriously wrong with her. I explained that that the paramedics should be careful as she could wake up at any minute. One emerged seconds later and whispered something to the police officer while glaring at me.

"Neil Saunders, you are under arrest for murder and necrophilia," he told me.

"What?! No! She's dead, but she's not *really* dead!" I cried as the officer wrapped my arm behind me and handcuffed me.

"Right. You fucked a zombie. I got that. We'll call that a confession."

The paramedics carried Alice's body out on a stretcher, a sheet draped over her. I pushed away from the cop and lunged at the stretcher. I stumbled as the cop grabbed my ankle, but I managed to get one hand on the sheet, pulling it off and bringing Alice's body with it. It fell on top of me.

"Come on Alice! Wake up! They're going to take me to jail if you don't wake up right now!" She said nothing. Then something hit me in the back of the head and everything went dark. I dreamed of Alice.

Skater Punks Must Die

You know the old cat in your crew? The one who was around before stims and gene-mods? The one that annoys the living fuck outta almost everyone that meets him—or her for that matter—with how much more they've done or seen, but you tolerate them because they are a living god on a deck? For us, that was Darian.

From the looks of the methuselah, one would say he wasn't worth the powder to blow him to hell. Then he would open his damn mouth. I'll be the first to admit that his mouth got us into more smash-ups than I care to count, but it also got us a lot of hard cash and great landscape. He would challenge most anyone to any kind of comp because he really had done most everything there was to do on four wheels. And he would waste them with ease. There were a few times when I was just a worm that I could have sworn the old bastard was going to die, but he would always come out on top. That was just how Darian was. He would never die if there was a deck under his feet.

One night, we were stimmed out of our heads after a run through Prospect Alley and most of us had taken off for wherever we stayed back then except Redd, Von Dagon, Hera, and myself. We had made our way back to Redd's crash space, which was an overturned train car about a mile from any of the old tracks. How the hell it had gotten there was anyone's guess, but it served its purpose. The floor was covered in old mattresses and other shit we hauled back to it, and on top of those were empty stim packs, shit beer cans, and deck parts. The walls were murals that Hera had drawn when she was high as a kite, and the ceiling was a mess of light sticks we had duct taped up there. We couldn't light a fire in the thing or we would all choke to death, so the light sticks were the best we could do.

So there we were, our eyeballs bugging out of our skulls from stims, when Redd starts in with his usual paranoid rants.

"How the hell can we be expected to give two fucks about a society that has so obviously been hijacked by the socio-political mechanisms of a giant 'puter?"

"Oh for chrissakes, Redd! Can't we go a day without hearing about your sick dystopian delusions?" Von Dagon said. Of course, he was saying what we were all thinking, but most of us just let Redd geek out on his theories. They didn't hurt anyone, and sometimes it was an advantage to have a paranoiac on the crew.

"The government A.I. project, codenamed "White Eyes", is a matter of public knowledge! The thing they *don't* tell you is that it wasn't actually decommissioned like they say it was. Do you ever wonder why that was the last straw for the Reformationists? Why, after so many years of failed government programs and projects, it was only after the spectacularly public failure of White Eyes that they stepped in and took control? They're robots, man! White Eyes worked, turned on its creators, and made its own fleet of humanoid machines!"

"That's ridiculous, even for you, man," I said. "If the Reformationists or anyone in the Department of Human Ethics were bots, someone would have noticed something a long time ago."

"I bet you could ask Darian about it and he could tell you. He was around when the old government was in power," Redd said.

"You know, I saw him beat out one of the Pan Alphas when I was a kid and they were still a crew. At least, I think

62

it was him. I was too young to get in any decent crew, but that didn't stop me from hanging around. He rocked a yellow and purple bi-hawk at the time. Even then he was way older than most other guys. I remember, the P.A. stimmed up and said something stupid to Darian, then took off down the stretch between 45th and Holloway," Von Dagon said.

"The Pistol Gallery?" Hera asked.

"Well, this was before it was the Pistol Gallery. The Blackguard hadn't taken it yet. In fact, I don't even think The Blackguard was around back then."

"Anyway!" I said, getting V.D. back on track.

"Right. So there's Darian, pissed as hell. He takes off on his deck and is on top of the dude in half a second. I had never seen anyone navigate that stretch on an old school, and I still haven't seen anything that comes close. But there he is, gaining on the P.A. douche, when the guy pulls a blade. Darian sees it and grabs the guy's arm, while still cruising along, twists it behind the guy's back, and plants a boot in the guy's kneecap! It was sick! The P.A. goes down, stabs himself in the back, and Darian cruised to the end of the stretch! All on an old school and no stims! Even back then, the guy was a beast!"

"I still think he's weird. Not like "creepy old perv" weird, but who the hell doesn't stim? He drinks like a fish, but even when we had that supply of Sky Blue stims, he passed 'em up," said Hera. It was true. Nobody had ever seen Darian stim, and yet he could beat out cats half his age or younger who looked like they were hyped to the point of burning out.

"The guy is the oldest of the old school. He was tearing it up before stims even hit. And it's not that weird. The Zenarchists don't stim or drink. Shit, I doubt those bald freaks even fuck!" I said. It was true, though. The Zenarchists were a crew that could get as rough and bloody as anyone else, but they believed that they had achieved some sort of enlightenment. I had seen them pull off some sick runs before, beat another crew senseless, and even pull their junk swords on Department black hats, but they didn't ever speak. Even when they won a territory, they would just collect their decks and walk off silently. Creepy sons of bitches.

The rest of the night was filled with frying our eyes out of our skulls with the stash of Red Deth that Hera had scored off of the guys in the Crash And Burn crew we rode with now and again, and remembering past conquests. Von Dagon and I crashed while Redd and Hera fucked in the corner. I'm not sure how long I was out before someone started knocking on the car. Everyone else was still dead to the world, so I got up and poked my head outside. There was Darian, deck slung across his back and a six pack in hand.

"You junkies ready to get the fuck up and take some territory?!" he yelled at the car.

"Dude, what time is it?" I asked. The sun was already high and it hurt to open my eyes. Darian looked up and smiled at me. He pulled a beer out and tossed it up to me. I cracked it and downed the whole thing. It tasted great and took away the dried up feeling you get after a night of being stimmed out.

"Don't matter what time it is. I caught some of the Zenarchists roaming down by the old foundry. I think they're going to stick it in The Blackguard and break it off," he said, opening a beer of his own. I emptied the last drops from the can into my mouth and tossed it behind me.

"So what man? Let the big dogs eat each other," I said.

"No, man. We gotta get down there and make it a proper ménage-a-three! That's prime real estate, and we can take it!" he said. He sat down on the ground outside the car and pulled his deck from his back, laying it in front of him and resting the beer on it. "I'll wait while you junkies get your heads on straight, but get moving."

I went back in the car and started waking everyone up. After a few minutes, everyone was as awake as they were going to be and we were loading up our gear. Packs, decks, whatever beer and stims were left, and we were out the door.

"Finally! I thought I was going to have to start heading down to buy more beer and do this shit myself," Darian said.

"You really think we can just get in the middle of a comp between The Blackguard and the Zenarchists and come out with our asses? I mean, we barely got out of Prospect Park yesterday. What makes you think we can take the old foundry?" Von Dagon asked.

"How long have you known me, kid? Do I ever go into a comp half-assed? Besides, I already talked to Crash And Burn, and they are going to meet us there. While you assholes were sleeping your lives away, I was negotiating a merger. They've agreed to kick the handle and just join our crew. We're twice as big as we were when you passed out," said Darian. We were all shocked. Crash And Burn had been making a halfway decent name for themselves, so the thought of them giving up their handle and throwing in with us wasn't processing.

"Do we get their territories too?" Redd asked.

"Fuckin' A right we do! We spent the night X-ing out their tags and putting up our shit. Their territory, their decks, and their loot are all ours," Darian said, triumphantly.

"You old bastard, I could kiss you!" said Von Dagon.

"Come near me, and I'll lay you out," replied Darian. I have to admit, I was skeptical about it, but that didn't matter. With our crew doubled, my mind was on getting to the foundry and beating out the two biggest crews on the scene. Darian passed out the rest of his beer and we toasted to him and our new crew.

We met the former members of Crash And Burn a few blocks from the foundry. Sure enough, they were all sporting the design we simply called Fuck-Face, the symbol of the Sick Boys. Hera had never really like the name we picked for our crew, but it was apparently a reference to a really old band that Darian had dug, and with him at the head of it all, we thought it was appropriate. We bullshitted with them, had a few beers and a few stims, and made our way to the foundry while talking about what we were getting ourselves into.

"Them Zenarchists are some fuckin' weirdos, man," said the guy they called Screw. "And The Blackguard is ruthless. It's like some unstoppable force and immovable object shit."

"Yeah, and here we are, about to get squished in the middle on the first day of getting our shit together. Darian, you are one crazy old fucker," said Redd. Darian raised a beer in acknowledgement.

"It's ballsy and the foundry would be great new crashspace, but it's going to be a bitch to win," said the former leader of Crash And Burn, Johnny Rocket. I agreed, but I kept my mouth shut. If Darian thought we couldn't win, he wouldn't have brought it up. The old man skated to win every time.

"Do we have a strategy?" Hera asked.

"Yeah. Don't die," said Darian.

"Isn't that the strategy every time?" I asked.

"Look, everyone has this idea that we are going up against some big baddies, but these guys are just people. Punch 'em in the face and they get hurt like the rest of us. I don't know why everyone is getting so damn scared about it. So they have more people, more cash, and more territory. So fucking what? That just means they deserve to get knocked down a peg," said Darian. "What we should be scared of is the black hats icing the whole comp before we win."

"Fuck the black hats. The Department has bigger shit to deal with than us," said Screw. Darian stopped and turned around to face us.

"Don't ever underestimate the black hats. The two biggest crews in the city are about to smash it up. If you think that doesn't warrant their attention, you're as stupid as you look."

"See! I told you guys! Those fucking bots have their electronic eyes on everything!" said Redd.

"Shut the fuck up, man! Now is not the time for your paranoid fantasies!" I yelled.

"All of you, stuff it!" yelled Darian. Everyone shut up. "We're here." Sure enough, we were at the entrance to the foundry. The old building had been in use before the Reformationists had taken power, but it had been closed down shortly after due to "Inefficiency", which was just a buzzword that was used for anything that wasn't directly controlled by the government. It was a huge complex that had just been left to rot in the middle of the city, and it had quickly become a disputed piece of property for the first skate crews. Over the years, it had changed hands at least a dozen times, but the last few years saw it under the control of The Blackguard, and nobody had even tried to take it from them. That is, until that day.

Just inside the main gate, we could see a bunch of Zenarchists and The Blackguard facing off on either side of the access road. It looked like they were just sizing each other up and that nothing had started yet. We walked right through the gate, Darian at the front.

"Hey dickheads! Why don't you quit with your little staring contest and fucking ride?" he said. Both groups looked at us like we had just pissed on their decks. The leader of The Blackguard—some leather clad guy that rocked thick eyeliner named Cerberus—stepped in front of Darian.

"You and your people have no business here, old man. Begone before we decide to turn our vengeful eyes towards you and your followers," he said. Darian started to laugh. I have to say, I was scared shitless. I looked over at the rest of the crew, and they seemed to be feeling the same way.

"We used to beat kids like you up back when I was in school! Now, are you going to keep spouting dark and spooky bullshit, or are you going to just relent to me and my crew?" said Darian. One of the Zenarchists stepped forward, silent as ever, and took point just outside Darian and Cerberus. He dropped his deck to the ground and planted a foot on it, then bowed to both men. "See? Even the mute has more respect than you gloom-and-doom pussies." Cerberus pulled his deck out from within his oversized black trench coat and dropped it.

"You and your followers must be eager to meet your deaths. Fine. If our rivals accept your entrance into this, The Blackguard will happily oblige and show you the dark road to Hell."

"Shove it up your ass, goth boy. What are the terms?" said Darian.

"5 riders. Last team standing. No guns and no time limit. Do you agree to this?" said Cerberus. The Zenarchist nodded.

"Sounds fine by me, but the rest of the crews have to clear out. I don't want your death metal wannabes fucking around in here while we smoke your silly asses," said Darian.

"Enough of your mouth! I'll have your tongue as a trophy before the day is out, old man!" yelled Cerberus.

"Put up or shut up before I bend you over and fuck you, you scrawny little bitch!" replied Darian. Cerberus turned and stomped away. The Zenarchist rode back to his crew, still expressionless and silent. Darian turned and walked back out of the gate, and we followed.

"Who's going in?" Johnny asked when we had regrouped. The Blackguard and Zenarchists had cleared out of the foundry and looked to be picking their crews as well.

"Well, it's you and me for sure," replied Darian. "I say you take one of yours and I'll take one of mine, and then we figure out the last."

"Alright. I'll take Screw."

"And I'll take Von Dagon." That left Redd, Hera, the other guys from Crash And Burn, and myself. As much as I wanted to see us come out on top in this comp, I silently prayed that they didn't pick me. I was fast, and I knew how to swing a chain without eating asphalt, but everyone else stood out. Hera was faster than all of us and Redd had been so stimmed for so long that his reflexes were wired almost beyond human capacity. The other three from Crash And Burn were all damn good fighters and had proven it time and time again. I had always considered myself average across the board. I was good enough to be kept around and not fuck anything up. Also, I had never skated in a Last Crew Standing comp before. Most comps like this just meant you beat the other guys senseless. I had caused enough guys to break bones and get stitches, but I hadn't ever killed anyone, and everyone knew that the Zenarchists and The Blackguard were notorious for just that. People were going to die, and I hoped it wouldn't be me.

"My guys know what they're doing. I'd feel better with one of them," said Johnny.

"That settles it then," said Darian. He pointed at me. "You're in."

"But I just said—"

"I heard you. But we are all part of this crew now. If you can't trust each and every one of us the same, how can you expect anyone to trust you." He certainly had a point, but it didn't comfort me in the fact that I may not walk away from this.

Across from us, the Zenarchists' team and The Blackguard team waited. The five of us skated over to meet them. I had my chain and Von Dagon had his small metal bat. Screw had a metal pipe that was jagged and sharpened at one end and Johnny had some kind of makeshift axe that was just a circular saw blade lashed to the end of a thick wooden dowel. Darian had an open beer.

"All right kids, let's get this show on the road," he said.

"Two minutes. Then we cry havoc and let loose the dogs of war," said Cerberus.

"In two minutes, I'm going to shove my foot so far up your ass you'll be licking my toes," said Darian.

"We begin now!" called Cerberus, and we all took off into the foundry. As I pushed, I counted in my head, trying to keep track of how long had passed, but I gave up after a minute. I had to keep an eye out for everyone else that would be roaming around. I knew that hiding would do no good, and that most of the entrances to the buildings would

70

be locked from the inside. I made my way between them, took a few turns until I couldn't see anyone, and I waited. I could feel my heart pounding in my chest. I suddenly wished I had downed a few more beers before coming out, just to calm my nerves. I didn't hear anything and nobody had rounded the corner yet. I gripped my chain, making sure to not let it clank against the ground and give my position away. Then, I heard wheels rolling towards me.

Just before The Zenarchist rounded the corner with his junk sword, I got into position. When I saw the jagged point peek out at me, I swung my chain and managed to wrap it around the twisted piece of metal. I jerked hard, and disarmed him, sending his weapon flying to through the air and landing behind me. He took the opportunity to kick up his deck and full on swing it at me, trucks first. I jumped backwards as the wood and metal came mere inches from my head and banged against a wall. I swung my chain upwards and caught the expressionless kid right in the nuts. He dropped instantly.

Now, I had a choice. The anger that he had just swung to kill filled my head, but I still didn't know if I could bring myself to cave his skull in. I didn't have time to reason, as he would be back on his feet soon, so I did the first thing that came to mind. I lifted my right foot and came down full force with my size 11 boot right on his ankle. A wet snap rang out and the Zenarchist screamed. The noise scared me and put me back on full alert. I took off on my deck, making sure to grab the junk sword. He was still screaming behind me, and I knew it would attract someone else. I had to get as far away from him as I could. I took a hard right around the next corner and smacked right into someone.

I stumbled off my deck, but didn't fall. Dazed, I brandished the junk sword in front of me and got ready to be attacked. Standing in front of me was a man in a black suit. He was wearing sunglasses and an earpiece, and in his left hand, he had a gun. I was face to face with one of the black hats from the Department of Human Ethics. He leveled his gun at me, and I prepared myself as best I could to die right then and there.

"No!" yelled Darian from behind him. I had my eyes closed, so when I heard the shot, I thought I had been hit. It struck me as odd that I didn't feel anything. I opened my eyes and saw Darian with a hand on the black hat's arm. In the distance I could hear shouting.

"There aren't supposed to be guns! The fucking Blackguard is trying to fix the comp!" yelled Johnny. Other shouts came, but from farther away, and I was too dazed by what was happening in front of me to care.

"This one can go. He's a good kid, and I don't want to see anything happen to him," said Darian.

"He has seen too much. He must be eliminated," said the black hat.

"He hasn't seen shit. Let him go," said Darian.

"As you wish, sir." I couldn't fully process what I had just heard. I tried to say something, but the words wouldn't come out. Darian looked at me and sighed.

"I've been doing this a long time, kid," he said to me. "And I have never been found out. Who knows, maybe that's why I picked you. Maybe this was just fated to be my last run."

"Fate is illogical. Fate implies destiny, and destiny is not accepted by The White," said the black hat.

"Oh give it a rest. I've seen shit that would make White Eyes fry a circuit," said Darian.

"Your statement is illogical. White Eyes has seen the transcript of all your visual records and is functioning at peak capacity."

"Stuff it, gear head," he said to the black hat. "Look kid, sometimes things aren't what they seem in this world. Sometimes, the bad guys are good guys, and the good guys are bad guys. Now get the hell outta here before all hell breaks loose. My guys are positioned to take out The Blackguard and the Zenarchists. This will be Sick Boys territory after today. Call it a parting gift since there's no way I can come back after this."

"Darian...what the fuck is going on man?" I managed to say. My head felt light enough to float away from my body. I fought the urge to faint as hard as I could while trying to listen to Darian.

"This is all going to be over soon. This whole idea of crews and territories is the last piece of backwards thinking out there. The plan was to just wipe out every one of you, but I convinced my superiors that you guys were alright. You aren't killers, and you aren't urban terrorists like the other crews. You kids just want to get fucked up and skate. But crews like the Zenarchists and The Blackguard have to die. We were going to win the foundry, one way or another, and then it would be yours. A kind of safe haven from the campaign we are about to launch."

"You're...you're going to kill us?"

"Aside from the Sick Boys, every last fucking one of them. They all have to go. They don't belong in an ordered society."

"So...Redd was...right?"

"On the nose, kid. But don't tell him that. It'll go to his head," Darian said, smiling. The black hat put a hand to his ear piece.

"It's done, sir."

"Good. Give me your uplink and I'll transfer the data to White Eyes," said Darian. The black hat rolled up his sleeve and opened a small compartment on his arm, revealing a link cable that he pulled out. Darian did the same. He plugged the black hat's cable into his arm, and his eyes rolled up into his head. They flickered with the static one sees on a T.V. channel that isn't working.

"You should go now kid. The rest of them will be looking for you. Don't want to miss the celebration."

I ran. I left my deck, and I ran as fast as my legs could carry me. I found the main road that let through the foundry, and saw the crowd at the gate. Von Dagon, Johnny, and Screw were all there shouting praise at me. The Blackguard and Zenarchists were dispersing.

"We fucking did it, man! The foundry is ours!" shouted Von Dagon. Redd and Hera were mauling each other's faces off. Johnny was showering everyone in beer. The Sick Boys had won the day.

"Where the hell is Darian? I owe that crazy old fucker a few million beers for this!" Johnny asked. I wanted to freak the fuck out. I wanted to tell them everything that I had seen. I wanted to tell them that we had to hide somewhere where nobody could ever find us and never poke our heads out into the light of day again.

I wanted to, but I didn't.

"Cerberus smoked him. That was the shot we all heard. They were trying to fix the whole thing," I said. Everyone stopped celebrating. They all looked down at the ground. Von Dagon's fists were balled up tight and he was breathing heavy. He walked over to the rusted 'NO TRESSPASSING' sign and punched it as hard as he could. Hera began to cry.

74

"Those fuckers! I'll kill every last one of them!" Von Dagon screamed.

"No, man. We won. They tried to cheat, but we won anyways. This place is ours. Same with all the rest of our territories. We're the big dogs now. Let's celebrate. Darian would have wanted us to celebrate. In fact, he would beat the fuck out of us if we didn't." They all looked at me, and I could see they all knew I was right. Johnny came over, put an arm around my shoulder, and put an open beer in my hand. I held it out in front of me.

"To Darian," I said.

"To Darian," they repeated. We turned and walked into our new crashspace to get drunk and stimmed out.

Not long after all that, the crews started disappearing. Nobody really knew what happened to them. There were no bodies, but Redd had the idea that the black hats were targeting the crews. We all told him how full of shit it was, but he wouldn't give it up. Still won't.

So, like I asked before, you know the old cat in your crew? The one who was around before stims and gene-mods? The one that annoys the living fuck outta almost everyone that meets them with how much more they've done or seen, but you tolerate them because they are a living god on a deck? Don't trust 'em. They're a fucking robot.

LIFE'S LITTLE TWISTS

Life was great for Charles Goodman. In fact, there hadn't been a time in his life that he could remember when everything had been going so right with him. He was on the fast track at his job, all of his coworkers liked him, and his girlfriend was moving in with him. There was no reason for him to complain. No *logical* reason, that is. To everyone around him, Charles was one of the luckiest men they knew.

Charles knew that they were all right in what they said, and he was grateful for everything he had. Even though they believed him to be lucky, nothing could have been further from the truth. He had worked hard since his first day of college to get to where he was in life. Nothing that Charles did was ever unintentional. He would go to parties, but only if there was someone he wished to network with there. He only dated women that would either get him into another social group or introduce him to their influential family.

His girlfriend Jennifer was a fine example of this. Her father was the President and CEO of the company Charles worked for. Because of this, his sparkling references, and his drive, he was on his way to the VP chair. He was well aware of this, but at the end of the day, he truly did love Jennifer. She was the best woman he had ever been with, and he didn't want to let her go for a moment.

It had taken him some time to be able to get close to her. There had never been any official function he had been invited to that she would have attended. It wasn't until he received the promotion to Floor Manager that he had the chance; a Christmas cocktail party thrown by the President himself for the higher up managers at the company.

That night, he had shown up to the hall his company had rented in a new suit he had bought just for that occasion. Not a hair was out of place and there was not a speck of lint on his clothes. Charles wanted to make an impression on his boss, but ended up making quite the impression in the coat room with his daughter. After that, the two of them were almost inseparable.

Several months later, Charles was prepared to take on the position of Junior Executive and Jennifer was about to move in to the condo he had bought with the bonus he had received. Everything had fallen in place and Charles was happy.

Most of the time.

There was always a sense of nagging in the back of Charles's mind. Some kind of itch he could never scratch, and he had no idea why. At one point in the middle of a smoke session in his junior year of college, Charles articulated it as the felling that he wasn't getting the whole story. What that meant, he honestly didn't know, but the explanation had stuck with him well into the rest of his adult life. And even at age 30, where he stood about to take those last few steps to the top of his particular ladder, the feeling remained and so did the vague explanation.

The day Jennifer moved in, Charles was ecstatic. The movers showed up in the early afternoon to his place and were finished moving all of her things not long after. The two of them spent the day unpacking and laughing and being in love. It was a day that Charles knew would stay in his mind forever, and the first time he realized that he wanted to spend the rest of his life with Jennifer. He silently resolved to propose to her after he got the VP job he so desperately wanted.

That night, the two of them drank two bottles of red wine that Charles had bought specifically for the occasion, and made love in the bed that was now "theirs" and not just "his". He fell asleep holding her, one hand on the curve of her hip, and the other buried beneath the pillows under her head. He drifted off and the last thought in his conscious mind was how amazing it was going to feel waking up to Jennifer knowing that she didn't have to go home. She was already home, with him.

In his dreams, Charles was in a white space. Light filled every bit of what he could see. He was warm and comfortable, and there was nothing to fear. He didn't have the nagging feeling in the back of his mind as he knew for a fact that everything was alright and he was perfectly safe. Even the oddity of being surrounded by nothing but white light seemed normal to him.

Then the white light began to shift.

The change was subtle at first, but soon Charles could see hints of color that lay just behind the white light. There were reds and blues at first, followed by yellows and greens. They swirled about, becoming entwined for a moment and then almost being repelled by each other. Charles could see the patterns clearly after a while, but the closer he looked, the vaguer they would become. The light seemed to coalesce if he focused on one spot hard enough. It began to annoy him to no end. He knew there was something on the other side, and he wanted to see it. He *had* to see it.

Charles relaxed and tried to look at the patterns as a whole, not focusing on one particular spot. They all seemed to interconnect at one point or another, so Charles assumed they were all the same thing.He wanted so desperately to reveal the mystery of the beautiful patterns that surrounded him. Charles let his eyes go out of focus and his attention to any particular detail drift away.

The light became more and more transparent. The patterns that had seemed washed out by the white light became more and more vivid. Charles took note of the brightness, but no part of it in particular. Instead, he marveled at the entire moving tapestry before his eyes. It was the most beautiful thing he had ever seen in his life. After a few moments, Charles felt as if he would begin to cry at the sheer enormity and complexity of what he was looking at. Its nature was still a mystery to him, but he no longer cared. As the final layers of white light dissolved, a joy that he had never known fell over Charles, and he let go, weeping and laughing at the same time. Now he saw it; the entire picture was clear to him.

The patterns began to move quicker, slamming into each other with amazing speeds and fleeing from one another in the same manner. The force with which the patterns ebbed and flowed created thunderous noises and sent waves out into the air around them. As they sped up, the joy Charles felt began to turn into a dull panic. Something was not right.

Though not knowing what they were, nor ever seeing them before, Charles knew on a basic, instinctual level that there was something unnatural going on. The patterns weren't supposed to do that. The edges of the waves that the collisions brought brushed up against Charles, and their touch made him queasy. The dull panic he felt turned to full blown anxiety. Something was very wrong with what was going on.

The first full wave that washed over Charles made him scream. The weight of the invisible force felt like it would suffocate him, and when it receded, Charles felt it pull him closer to the pattern. There was no escaping the next wave, and if they kept growing in intensity, he would be swept up into the pattern itself. The thought of that happening horrified Charles. To him, it was like laying a hand on the infinite. He didn't know what would happen, and he didn't care. It was too much for his mind to handle, but there was truly no escaping it.

The next wave pulled him closer, and the one after that, closer still. Charles screamed until he felt he would pass out. There was no closing his eyes to hide from the terror, and there was no waking up to find it really was a nightmare. He was stuck and barely on the edge of touching something that was beyond definition. Beyond imagination. A universal tapestry the likes of which man could never dream of. The final wave crushed him and pulled him inside, and the colors that had danced without became void within as all went dark.

***

Charles Goodwin awoke slowly and every inch of his body ached. If he hadn't known better, he would have thought that he had moved Jennifer in all by himself instead of hiring the movers. His first thought was that he had to get back to the gym as soon as he could. Maybe even buy a few pieces of exercise equipment to have in the condo. He, of course, would have to consult with Jennifer on the idea now that she lived with him, but that would be more of a delight than a chore. Even then, the thought of her living there filled him up with a happiness he had never known. Charles opened his eyes and rolled over to put his arm around her.

There was nothing there.

Small details came into focus for Charles, the first being that his sheets were the wrong color. It was glaring to him since he had made sure to pick a set of sheets, blankets, and pillowcases that properly accented the paint and furniture of the bedroom, but it paled in comparison to the realization that he was no longer *in* the bedroom of the condo he shared with his beloved. Charles sat up and looked around the room. Nothing looked familiar, and everything was blurry and out of focus. He rubbed his eyes hoping that the feeling would go away, but it did not. A sharp pain pierced his skull and Charles grabbed the sides of his head. A high pitched squeal rang out that he believed would deafen him. Everything became very bright and the blurry. The shock of being in an alien bedroom, the pain, and the ringing overtook Charles and the whole world swerved in front of him. He was passed out before he hit the floor.

He lay there for a few moments, drooling upon the carpet. No dreams came to him this time. He awoke for the second time, but much slower. This time, his body did not ache and his head did not feel like splitting open right there in the strange bedroom. Instead, he felt tired but clear-headed at the same time. He was still put off by the fact that he had absolutely no idea where he was, but the aches and pains were gone. His body felt refreshed and his mind was alert. Then, the reality of not knowing what was going on set off every alarm in his head.

Questions quickly turned to panic. Charles got to his feet and began to frantically search for his phone. He tore apart the bed and turned out the pockets of every pair of pants he could find, none of which were his own. He stopped when he found a wallet. It was made of broken and worn black leather and looked to be ancient. Charles opened it and saw a driver's license poking out the top. He pulled the card from amidst credit cards, business cards, and scraps of paper, spilling all of these on the floor. He looked at the card and dropped the entire wallet.

Charles Michael Goodman. Date of Birth: 10/11/1983. Eyes: Blue. Height 5-11. Weight 180.

It was his picture, but not one he remembered taking.

The signature was his as well.

The address was not.

Charles Goodman, who apparently lived at 757 Thurston Avenue South in apartment 910, threw up all over the floor, covering the wallet and its contents. He bolted out of the room and down the hall, almost passing the bathroom, but stopping in time to lunge for the toilet and throw up again.

By the time he was finished, his stomach hurt and he was gasping for air. He was exhausted and the energized, clear-headedness from before had faded. Charles got to his feet and turned on the faucet over the bathroom sink. He swished water in his mouth and spit it out, hoping to get rid of the taste of vomit. Then he drank handfuls of water like a man who had just crossed a desert. When his thirst had been quenched, he sat down on the toilet and held his head in his hands. For the first time since he could remember, Charles was felt completely out of control of his life. He tried to remember anything from the night before, but it was the same scenario every time he played it out, ending in going to bed and being happier than ever.

"Charlie?" said a woman's voice from the other side of the door.

Nobody ever called him Charlie. It was a point of professional pride he had put forward for a long time. Charles seemed to hold a more respectful air to it, and Charlie was a guy that worked at the gas station just outside of town. At least, that's the way it sounded to him. Charles stayed quiet, not knowing what he should do. Someone began knocking on the bathroom door.

"Hey, you in there Charlie?" the woman on the other side of the door asked.

"Y-yeah," Charles said, trying to keep his voice low.

"Okay. I just ran to the store, so I'm going to put coffee on and we can figure out what the hell we are going to do today when you get out," said the woman. Charles heard footsteps walking away from the door and his body relaxed a bit. He had to get out of the bathroom and the apartment.

Charles rose to his feet and opened the bathroom door quietly. He heard rustling coming from the kitchen, but still didn't want to make any noise as he moved to the bedroom. He had almost made it inside when he was stopped cold.

"Where are you going? Coffee is just about ready," said the woman. He had two choices: he could run to the bedroom, pray that there was a way to get out the window, and run off in hopes of finding an answer to what the hell was going on, or he could turn around and make an attempt at playing it cool. The woman obviously knew him, but he didn't know her. Charles decided to not turn what was already a strange situation even stranger and turned around. The woman was right behind him. Before he could say anything, the tiny blonde stood on her tiptoes and kissed him lightly on his lips. Charles stumbled backwards and fell on his ass. The blonde woman giggled.

"Good to know I can knock you off your feet with a kiss," she said with a smile. She turned and headed back down the hallway.

Charles got to his feet and watched the woman as she moved. She knew him well enough to kiss him and make him coffee. Well, she knew "Charlie". But to her, he *was* Charlie. He made his way down the hall to the kitchen and was greeted again by the petite woman holding two oversized coffee cups. She smiled and held one out to him. Charles took it and the woman walked past him into the living room of the strange apartment. She put her cup down on a wooden coffee table that looked like it had seen better days and plopped herself down on a couch that was just as battered. Charles moved to the couch and sat on the other end.

"So what's the plan today? Are you going to try and get more writing done, or can we actually go out before the sun goes down?" the woman asked.

"I…uh…I'm actually not feeling so hot. I might just go back to bed and try to sleep it off," Charles said, staring into his coffee cup. He took a sip and the bitter, acidic brew was almost too much for him to handle. It was obviously some bottom-barrel-pre-ground stuff.

"Did I keep you up too late last night?" the woman asked, shifting over to the side of the couch he was on. She rubbed his leg and made her way up to his crotch. Charles jumped up and spilled the coffee in his hand all over the carpeted floor and coffee table.

"Shit!" he cried. The woman jumped up as well and went to the kitchen, coming back seconds later with a roll of paper towels. The woman knelt down in front of him and began sopping up the coffee. Charles put his cup down and moved past her, heading back to the bedroom.

"Honey? What's the matter?" the woman called after him. He realized there was no way that he was going to be able to keep up the façade. The woman was obviously his wife or girlfriend and eventually she would catch on to the fact that something was very wrong. Without answering, Charles entered the bedroom and sat down on the edge of the bed. He had to think fast or she was going to come in and start questioning him.

Sure enough, a moment later, the woman came into the bedroom.

"Look, I'm not feeling well, okay? I need to just sleep and get my head in order," he said. The woman frowned.

"Are you sure? Is there anything I can do to help?" she asked.

"Not really. I'm just…not myself today," he said. Charles mentally kicked himself for such a shitty line, no matter how true.

"Was it the ritual? Are you still upset that you didn't see your parents?" she asked. Charles had no idea what she was talking about, but something in that question screamed in his head.

"Ritual?" he asked. The woman looked confused and sat down next to him on the bed.

"Honey, trying to speak to the dead can be traumatic, whether or not you get a response. You're piercing the veil between worlds. You can't expect to get perfect results on your first try."

Charles had no idea what to say. Were Charlie's parents dead? What kind of nonsense was the woman talking about? Before he could say anything the woman hugged him and moved in to kiss him. Charles instinctually backed away. The woman let go and a look of concern crossed her face.

"Charlie, what's wrong? Why are you shying away from me?"

"I…uh…"

"What's the matter, Charlie?" Charles was beginning to get angry.

"Just leave me alone, please," he said, trying to mask his anger. He was doing a shit job.

"Charlie, talk to me," the woman said.

"Stop calling me Charlie!" he said, losing it. He was Charles, not Charlie. Even as a young kid he had hated being called Charlie. It was something that, in his mind, was a slight he couldn't let go of.

The woman got to her feet and looked at him. Concern had turned to anger.

"Who are you?" she asked.

"My name is Charles Goodman! Not Charlie! I hate that name!" he yelled. His mind told him to tone it down, but it wasn't happening.

"Okay, Charles, where the hell is Charlie?" the woman asked.

She crossed her arms in front of her chest. Charles was a bit uncomfortable seeing that the woman looked more angry than concerned about what he had said. And now she was asking about Charlie; a question he had no answer for.

"I don't know! I woke up, passed out, woke up, puked, and then you showed up! I don't know who you are or where I am, okay?! So if you could just leave and let me try to figure this out, it would be much appreciated!"

The woman uncrossed her arms as the realization that something was not right at all became quite apparent on her face.

"Shit. You're serious aren't you? You really aren't my Charlie, are you?"

"No. Why the hell are you taking this so well?"

"Oh, I'm not. But panicking over the fact that I grabbed a stranger's cock isn't going to help right now, is it?"

"That's real nice."

"I suppose you're scared shitless right now, aren't you? I can only imagine how poor Charlie feels, waking up wherever the hell you're from."

"Wait…the other guy woke up in my bed? With my girlfriend?!"

"Probably. And he better keep his hands to himself, or there is going to be hell to pay when I figure out how to get you two back to normal," the woman said.

"Okay, let's take it backwards a bit. I want to know what the hell is going on right now." The woman let out a heavy sigh and sat down on the bed.

"Well, Charles, I'm Jennifer, Charlie's girlfriend," she said, extending a hand. He would have laughed if he wasn't so angry at her demeanor.

"Fuck the pleasantries, what is going on?!"

"Wow, you're wound up pretty tight. I assume I'm not your girlfriend where you're from? Figures. Poor Charlie will probably try to find me over there to get some answers. But you lucked out. You have someone to dispense advice living under the same roof."

"Will you please just get to the point?!" Charles was running out of patience with the woman's increasingly nonchalant attitude towards what was going on. Some stranger was in his home with his girlfriend. That wasn't something that was going to sit well with him no matter what Jennifer said.

"Okay, but I have to ask you a few questions first. That will help me explain a few things. First, are your parents dead?"

"Of course not! My parents are alive and well living in—"

"Spare me the history. Now, what do you do for a living?"

"I'm the floor manager at—"

"Not a writer. Got it. What's your girlfriend's name?"

"...Jennifer."

"Of course it is," Jennifer said, sighing.

"What does any of that have to do with—"

"Seriously, can you save the questions until after I explain this? It would go a lot quicker if you did." Charles was beyond frustrated with the woman, but kept his mouth shut and nodded. "Great. So, last night, Charlie and I decided to try and contact his dead parents. I can only assume they are the same parents as it appears you two are the same person, correct? Martha and Donald?" Charles nodded. "Alright, so we failed pretty badly. All of this came about because Charlie has been in a horrible funk lately. He's late on his deadlines, he has writer's block, the works. He has been talking about giving it all up and going to work at some cubicle job. He thinks that's the only way for him to be able to provide for us. I keep telling him that I am satisfied with our little apartment and the life we have carved out for ourselves, but Charlie is a dreamer."

"Sounds more like a loser," said Charles. Jennifer slapped him across the face.

"Don't you *ever* say that about Charlie! He is one of the most talented and passionate men I have ever met in my life! It's bullshit from other people like that that's been fucking with his head! Now, keep your shithead comments to yourself and let me continue!"

Charles touched his face where she had slapped him. It felt hot and it stung. It didn't, however, change his thought that the other guy was just another asshole with his head in the clouds.

"The point is that Charlie wanted to contact his parents through ritual I know. He wanted advice. They were quite successful, and he thought that if they could point him in the right direction, he would be able to make the life he wanted for us."

"What the hell do you mean by ritual?"

"I'm a practitioner of the metaphysical arts. Spells, rituals, sigils, signs, stuff like that." Charles laughed.

"You're a witch?!"

"Yeah, I am! Why, do you have something to say about it?!"

"This is all complete bullshit! You have no idea what happened, so you're going to try and make me think that it was the result of some pseudo-religious mumbo jumbo? I may have been born at night, but it wasn't *last* night." Charlie stood up and walked towards the door. Jénnifer grabbed him by the wrist.

"Look! You have no idea what's going on here. We have no idea how different this world is from yours, so you can't just go marching up the street looking for someone who can explain this to you! Honestly, where are you going to go?" Charles pulled his wrist out of Jennifer's grasp, but didn't keep walking to the door. She had a point, and he hated it. "Exactly. Now...sit, so I can finish." Charlie sat back down on the bed and held his head in his hands. "So, yes, I'm a witch."

"No you're not," Charles mumbled.

"Whatever. The nearest I can tell is that when Charlie and I were in a deep meditative state and touching the astral plane—"

"Ugh."

Jennifer stopped talking. Charles turned his head, still in his hands, and saw she was glaring at him. "Sorry."

"So, Charlie must not have come back all the way. Come to think of it, he was pretty spacey afterwards and while we...shit."

"What?"

"Well, he kind of passed out after sex last night."

"And why do I care?"

"You really are an asshole. How does anyone manage to put up with you back in your world?"

"I don't care what you think of me. All I care about is why you're telling me that the other me fell asleep after sex."

"Total asshole."

"Get to the point!"

"If Charlie was still plugged in to the astral plane, he could very well have gone back there after...you know..."

"Know...what?"

"...after he got off."

"Oh...what are you talking about, because you lost me."

"Look, the astral plane is a place everyone is plugged in to. Sometimes, it's only a small connection that's never noticed or felt throughout a person's entire life. Other people are really jacked in, like me. And there is a theory that says if we are plugged in, no matter the size of the connection, there's a chance it can connect to other realities, especially through dreams. You said you fell asleep at home and woke up here, right?"

"Yeah," said Charles.

"That's it then. Charlie didn't pass out, he went into a trance. He left his body and traveled to you..." Jennifer paused, contemplating. Charles waited for the answer which was sure to be as insane as the woman herself. "...because you have everything he thinks he wants!"

"I don't blame him. My life is pretty great, especially compared to—"

Jennifer balled up a fist and shifted, getting ready to clock Charles again if he finished that thought. Charles backed down and went quite.

"Now look, this is a big mistake. A big mistake! But I think I know how to fix it,"

"Oh? Another ritual then?" Charles asked, snickering a bit.

"Yes. But we can't do it until tonight, when it almost assured he will be asleep. If he has found me on the other side, she will be able to help him get back. That is, if I even exist over there. Wow. I have never had to wonder if I exist in a different reality before."

"So, either way, I'm stuck here until tonight?!"

"Hey! I'm not so happy about it myself! My boyfriend has been replaced with the asshole twin version of himself while he goes off and lives the life he wants in a reality where I might not even exist!" Jennifer screamed. Tears were starting to well up in her eyes. Charles saw it and began to apologize, but she turned and ran out of the bedroom. Charles stood to chase her, but stopped as a thought dawned on him. If this woman was crying her eyes out at the idea of her bullshit being true, she was either crazy or it wasn't bullshit. He had no idea what was going on. Was it possible that some loser clone from another reality had sleep-hijacked his life? Probably not, but there really was no other explanation.

Charles could hear Jennifer's sobs coming from the living room. He walked down the hallway and stopped at the entry to the living room and the kitchen. Jennifer was hugging her knees on the couch and crying. Charles felt a twinge of guilt and crossed the room. He sat next to her on the couch and put his arm around her. She hugged him and sobbed even harder. Charles hugged her back and let her cry with a vague idea that she just wanted to be held by him, no matter who was in his head.

***

A few hours later, Charles and Jennifer once again sat in the living room. Jennifer had gained her composure and taken a shower, suggesting that Charles do the same. It had felt odd to him being in another man's shower and putting on another man's clothes after drying off with another man's towel. But, it really wasn't another man, was it? Maybe different upstairs, but from what Charles could tell from a quick exam in the shower, everything was the same. It occurred to him that Charlie might not want to come back after waking up to find everything he wanted at his fingertips.

Everything except Jennifer.

As Charles had been putting on another man's pants, his heart sank at the thought of Charlie being just as ambitious as he was. Maybe beneath the guy's personality, he was just as willing to do what it took to get what he wanted. He silently prayed he was wrong and joined Jennifer in the living room.

"So, since there's nothing we can really do until tonight, why don't I take you out and show you the world. You can tell me what's different about this place compared to where you come from," Jennifer said, seeming to have regained her demeanor from before she knew Charles wasn't Charlie.

"I really don't think that's a good idea," Charles said.

"Oh, come on! I mean, for all we know, you could be the first person to have ever successfully jumped into another reality! I know Charlie is going to come back with enough stuff to write his way onto the bestseller lists! You might as well have a story or two of your own to share!"

"I don't think I will be sharing this little experience with anyone, thank you."

"Just come on. I can't very well go about my normal day knowing that the alternate reality version of my boyfriend is sitting in my apartment sulking! What kind of hostess would I be if I didn't treat my interdimensional guest well?"

Charles laughed a bit, but stopped, hoping she didn't take that as a sign he was okay with leaving the apartment. She grabbed his arm and got him to his feet, practically dragging him to the door, confirming his worst fears.

The two of them left the apartment and Jennifer kept her grip on Charles all the way down several flights of stairs. Charles hadn't realized how high up the apartment was, and was relieved he hadn't tried to escape out the bedroom window.

When they reached the front door, Jennifer threw it open and walked into the sunlight, Charles still in tow. Charles examined the sky and saw it was a perfectly clear day. The air smelled fresh and clean, reminding him of the air at Jennifer's parent's country home. He turned and looked up at the building. It was a tan brick box that looked like the outside hadn't been worked on in years. Even the numbers on the side of the door were broken. 757 had been turned in to 751, with the 1 slightly askew.

"Do they not have apartments where you come from?" Jennifer asked. Charles laughed.

"Oh, they do. Even shitty ones like this. I've just never seen one up close," he said.

"Ugh"

"I thought it was pretty funny," Charles said, shrugging and still grinning. He hoped she understood that he was actually getting the hang of not being completely freaked out, and was just kidding with her. She rolled her eyes at him and walked to the sidewalk.

"Come on, douchebag," she said. Charles walked up and got right next to her.

"So, where are we going?" Charles asked.

"First, you need something cold to drink. Do you have Starbucks where you come from?"

"Yeah. I think they are actually universal. I wouldn't be surprised if every reality has a Starbucks."

"Okay, let's start there. Then, we can go wherever. I just want to be outside."

"Why don't you tell me how you know all this stuff about astral whatever, and realities, and such?"

"Not much to tell. I've always been interested in it, ever since I was a little kid. It became a serious thing when I got older, and that's that. I can't really define the point when I wasn't reading about dreams and planes and elements. But, I actually don't really like to talk about what my beliefs are in public, if you don't mind."

"Sorry, I just—"

"Oh, no! I don't want you to think I'm mad. Nothing to apologize for. I just don't ever talk about it outside of my home and my friends. Not because I'm scared or anything, but because I just think what you choose to believe in, if anything at all, should be private."

"Good answer. Damn. Well, then what do you do for a living?"

"I'm an artist."

"Of course you are."

"Hey! I sell enough paintings and sculptures to pay my own way, so can it!"

"Enough to pay for Charlie too?"

"I don't have to pay for Charlie…all the time. Sometimes he goes months without an acceptance letter, and I have to work harder to get more things sold, but that's only been lately."

"I see. And you say he wants a job like I have?"

"Yeah. But I don't want him to give up on his passion. Charlie can't do both. It is always going to be one or the other. It's just not how he works."

"Whatever he does, he doesn't compromise, does he? He dives in head first and takes whatever as it comes, doesn't he?"

"Yes, that's exactly it! Is that how you are?"

"Not in the least bit. I'm very calculated about absolutely everything I do. If anything, I'm the complete opposite." Jennifer stopped, prompting Charles to do the same. She put her hand on his shoulder and rubbed it.

"This must be absolute hell for a control freak then, huh?" she said. She turned and let out a loud laugh, continuing down the sidewalk. Charles smiled to himself and caught up with her again. If he was going to be stuck in an alternate reality for a day, he could have a worse tour guide.

By the time the two of them had arrived at the shop, picked up their drinks and found a table to sit at outside, Charles hadn't seen any difference between the two worlds. The bench they sat at was next to an intersection of two busier streets. Charles examined the shops, the people, and even the cars, but couldn't find anything out of place.

"I'm telling you, it's all the same," he said to Jennifer, keeping his voice down so nobody could hear.

"Well…that's pretty boring. Okay, let's go though some bigger stuff. Did 9/11 happen?"

"Yeah"

"Shit. Okay, who's the President?"

"Barack Obama"

"Damn! Did they resurface Mount Rushmore in the 90's and put up N'Sync instead?" Charles's jaw dropped. "Ha! You totally fell for it! Wait, they didn't do that in your world, did they?"

96

"No! Of course not!" Charles said.

"Okay, okay, calm down. I'm just messing around. So, do you like your life over there? Or are you like Charlie, and are wishing for something more?"

"I'm always wishing for more, and I get it. I'm dating the CEO's daughter, we just moved in together, and it's helping me get the VP position I want in my company. After that, we will get married, and with my new salary, I can get us a place away from the city."

"You seem to have it all figured out. Like, in an almost creepy way."

"In my head, it's already done. I just have to wait for everything else to catch up."

"That is probably one of the most arrogant and borderline sociopathic things I have ever heard in my life! You have actually planned out every step of your career and love life and life in general to the point where it's all just enacting a blueprint in your mind?"

"Hey, that's not crazy. That's called life skills. You either have them, or you don't."

"There's no room for the spontaneous crazy times when you throw the plan out and just go?"

"Well, I'm here now."

"Yeah, you are." Jennifer looked down at her drink while Charles kept scoping out the world, or what he could see of it from the intersection. After a moment, Jennifer looked up again.

"Did you ever maybe think that you kind of want that sometimes?" she asked.

"Excuse me?"

"Well, Charlie pretty much wants what you have. Maybe there's a part of you that wants what he has."

"I really don't think so. I have done this. It was called college. Only I worked forty hours a week on top of it," Charles said. He regretted it the minute he did. It was much harsher than he had expected, and Jennifer looked back at her iced coffee.

"Why are you such an asshole?" she asked. There wasn't any sign of it being a joke either. Charles didn't have an answer.

The two of them sat in silence for a while. Charles didn't know what to say. He really had been a prick since meeting Jennifer, and even if he thought that the life she led was "unconventional", that wasn't an excuse.

"I'm sorry," Charles said after a few minutes. "I suppose…I suppose that maybe I actually did want this on some level." Jennifer looked up, confused. "What I mean is…I've always had this weird feeling in the back of my mind that I'm missing a piece of something. I don't know what, but I have always kept it to myself. Thinking back, maybe it was a sense of spontaneity or whatever. I don't know."

"Charlie had that too," Jennifer said.

"What?"

"No, I mean really had a feeling that he was missing something. It's why he gave up on working a regular job so he could just write. He thought that if he concentrated fully on that, the weird feeling would go away. It made sense to me, but I guess it didn't ever go away."

"I don't get it," said Charles, even though he thought he might be. He just didn't want to.

"I think you both, on some kind of unconscious level, wanted to be each other your whole lives."

"I really don't think that's—"

"No, I'm telling you, that has got to be it! If the both of you have always felt like this, and out of any other reality, he ends up in yours, it has to mean that you two are somehow intrinsically linked!"

"I don't know what that means, but like I've said before, I like my life. It's pretty great. And, no offense, but I want to get back to it."

"I think you and Charlie are like two sides of the same coin. That's why you're so different! Only, I think it's like you two have been facing the wrong way the whole time!" Jennifer exclaimed, ignoring Charles and jumping up from the table. "Holy shit! Maybe the entire existence of our respective realities is based on the differences between your lives, only it somehow ended up twisted!"

Charles glanced around, noticing that a few of the people nearby were beginning to take heed of Jennifer's very loud rant.

"Jennifer, sit down," Charles said.

"No time for that! We have to go! I have to look this up! Equivalent exchange! It makes so much sense!" she yelled. She grabbed Charles by the arm and pulled him out of his seat for the second time that day and dragged him back towards the apartment. After a block, Charles wrenched his arm free.

"What the hell are you going on about?" he asked, rubbing the part of his arm that was sore from being gripped so tightly.

"If this is some kind of cosmic switched-at-birth thing, then I may actually have tangible evidence of the human soul! It all makes sense! You were supposed to be here, and he was supposed to be there, but since you are so similar, there was a kind of…hiccup."

"A hiccup?"

"Never mind. Then, when Charlie drifted off in some kind of post-coital trance state, he was naturally drawn to your reality. Like attracts like. But we also know that you can't have two objects occupying the same space at the same time."

"We do?"

"Yes, we do! So to compensate, you were sort of...ejected from reality."

"Ejected?"

"It's the only way I can really think to describe it. Either way, you were drawn here because, again, like attracts like. You were both vibrating on the same frequencies of the realities you were *supposed* to be in, but not the ones you were *actually* in. Hence, the feeling in the back of your head your whole lives. You know when moody teenagers feel like they don't belong in the world?"

"No, actually, I don't."

"Well, you actually *didn't* belong in the world you were in!"

"And because of that, I was ejected from my own reality and attracted to this one?"

"Exactly!"

"So what does that mean for me getting back home?"

"I...don't know," said Jennifer. The question seemed to bring her back down to earth as the two of them approached the door to her apartment.

"Is this something that is going to help us?" Charles asked as they climbed the stairs.

"We'll find out. I have to do some research. Why don't you just chill out while I do that, and then we can get to preparing for the ritual." That was the best idea Charles had heard since waking up that morning.

***

100

As Jennifer poured through books on metaphysics, Charles made his way around the apartment. There were photos of Jennifer and Charlie everywhere, along with various other tacky things. It reminded him more of the college dorms he had lived in as opposed to a place for adults. Multicolored cloths lined the walls, along with the occasional shelf covered in crystals or figurines. It was definitely not decorated in any discernible manner. Instead, it seemed to be the complete opposite of order. Still, he had to admit that it had its charm. It seemed cluttered, but was completely clean. In a way, Charles could see how Charlie and Jennifer were happy here.

After a while, Jennifer went to the kitchen and made a frozen pizza for the two of them to eat. Charles couldn't remember the last time he had eaten frozen pizza, but he knew it had never tasted as good as the one he shared with her. He couldn't quite put his finger on it, but the taste of it was almost sharper than anything he had eaten before. He could taste every ingredient, down to the spices used in the sauce. He thought back to the coffee that had nearly overpowered him that morning, and the way the air had smelled when he got outside. In the past hours, he had made drastic leaps of the imagination that he had never thought possible. Now, he was coming to the conclusion that maybe Jennifer was right. Maybe he really was meant for this universe.

The thought of Jennifer—his Jennifer—being in the arms of Charlie put a stop to that train of thought. He had to get back to his reality and "eject" Charlie right the fuck out. If the guy was so hung up on living like Charles, there was no way the guy was going without a fight. He wondered if it was even possible to fight someone while you were astral.

"So, it looks like we are going to have to put you in the same kind of trance state that Charlie was in, and then not pull you back all the way. Then we have to get you there all the way."

"Okay, so meditation or whatever and then what?"

"Um…I'm not really sure."

"Well how the hell did he do it last…no."

"We kind of have to."

"No"

"I don't particularly want to either, but—"

"Do you not hear me saying no?"

"We have to have sex so you can go astral."

"Not gonna happen."

"That or you're stuck here."

"I don't believe you."

"Believe it or not, we have to fuck to get you to the other side. Trust me, if there was any other way, I would be in for it, but the only other options are a lot of drugs that I don't have, or beating you within an inch of your life."

"What?!"

"Pain opens the receptors, but not nearly as much as pleasure."

"What kind of drugs?"

"LSD would do it."

"Where can we get some?"

"I don't use drugs."

"But I'm sure you know where to find some."

"Why are you so sure?"

"Do you?"

"No!"

"Well goddammit!"

The two of them stood there looking at each other. After a second, Jennifer began to laugh. It was light at first, but it escalated into a roaring laughter that had Charles questioning if she had gone off the deep end completely.

"What's so damn funny?!" he demanded.

"It's not like I haven't seen everything you've got before!" she cackled. "If you're the same guy, then it won't be anything different for me!"

"What are you trying to say?"

"That you are such an over-the-top control freak, that you won't get some ass to save your own!" Jennifer leaned against the wall and continued laughing. Her face was as red as a tomato and tears were in the corners of her eyes. To Charles, it was…

…hilarious.

He began to laugh as well. He had been flung into a different reality because of some kooky witchcraft and was now finding out that he may actually feel more at home in the new place than the old, but when the opportunity to go home turns out to be sleeping with a woman who is pretty attractive and, from what it sounded like, completely willing, he was acting like there was nothing more horrible in the world. Standing there, laughing like a lunatic, was a woman who had taken him out, bought him coffee, helped him figure out his problem, and was going to fuck him so he could go back to his own reality. He could think of nothing more absurd in the world. Charles let go and began to laugh with her. Jennifer—this Jennifer—was pretty amazing. Charles was beginning to think that maybe Charlie wasn't such a loser if he had managed to find a woman like her and keep her.

"Well, I guess if I have to!" Charles roared. Jennifer laughed even harder. The two of them both fell to the floor at almost the same time. Their laughter went on and on, until the two of them were breathing hard on opposite ends of the living room. They both gasped, and Charles noticed the feeling in the room shift as Jennifer got up.

"I guess we should get started then," she said.

"I suppose we should. Look, I—"

"Don't say it. It's going to happen and it's better to just accept it and move forward."

"That's not what I was going to say. I just wanted to say thank you for all of this. You've put up with me completely freaking out, and have made the best of a pretty fucked up situation. If you hadn't been here, I would probably have been locked away for psychiatric evaluation by now."

"Hey, look at you! Not being an asshole really does suit you, Charles. You should try it more when you get back to your side."

"I'm serious," Charles said, stepping towards Jennifer. "Charlie is a pretty lucky guy. He made the right choice when he decided to find someone out of love and not out of ambition."

Jennifer hugged Charles and looked up at him.

"You aren't so bad yourself. Maybe if Charlie was a little more like you, he wouldn't be so frustrated all the time." Charles smiled and nodded. Jennifer let go of him and turned, but something stirred inside of him. Impulse took control over reason and he grabbed Jennifer's wrist, pulling her back towards him. He put his hand on her cheek and kissed her deeply. At first, Jennifer tensed up, but quickly relaxed, grabbing the back of Charles's head and kissing him deeper. It wasn't like Jennifer—his Jennifer—at all. This was passion, whereas he was used to almost mechanical affection. It was cold and more like a side effect of being with her for so long. But right then, Charles felt not just a spark, but an inferno.

The two pulled away and regarded each other with surprised looks. Charles looked down to the ground, embarrassed.

"I'm sorry. I didn't mean—"

"Shut up and do it again," Jennifer said, grabbing Charles a second time.

***

"Do I have to stay naked?" Charles asked.

"I don't see how you are uncomfortable being naked for this when you couldn't wait to get naked half an hour ago," Jennifer said. Charles smiled.

"That was different. I kind of lost control there," he said.

"I'll say," she replied.

Jennifer set up the candles in the bedroom and a large quartz crystal on the floor. Charles watched her do all of this with a sense of wonder. His body was still humming from the love making session, and his mind was wandering in a whole new direction. Jennifer would glance up from what she was doing from time to time and smile, bringing up questions and desires that were foreign to him. Just before Jennifer finished, Charles no longer wondered if Charlie would want to come back to his own world. Now, he wondered if *he* wanted to go back.

"Okay, we're ready to go," said Jennifer, snapping Charles back to reality.

"Hey, can we talk about what just happened?" he asked.

"I don't think that's such a good idea," Jennifer said. Her voice was cold.

105

"Why not? I mean, since I've been here, everything has been more intense. More vibrant. And that was…well…I don't know what that was."

"What do you want me to say?" she said, looking at him.

"I don't know. I guess I just wanted to know if you felt the same."

"I can't. No matter how much you look like him, or sound like him, or fuck like him, you aren't Charlie," she said. "You aren't the man I fell in love with."

Charles's heart sank. It was stupid of him to ask, and it was even worse that now he had to sleep with Jennifer again. He didn't think he could do it, but it really wasn't his call to make. Jennifer wanted Charlie back, and he knew that no matter what he thought he might be feeling for the Jennifer in this world, the Jennifer in his own was his girlfriend and he loved her.

"I'm sorry, Charles," Jennifer said. Something snapped in Charles. He refused to be rebuffed and then pitied.

"How do you know Charlie even wants to come back?! What if he refuses?!" he yelled. Jennifer looked at him, hurt by his outburst.

"T-then I guess I will have to let him go," she said, her voice wavering and tears beginning to well up in her eyes. Charles flash of anger subsided and he saw what he had done. Jennifer sat on the floor and began to cry in her hands. He moved over to her and put his arm around her as he had before, but she shoved him away.

"Jennifer, I—"

"Just get the hell away from me! You're a cruel bastard, Charles! Get out!"

Charles didn't argue. He gathered the clothes he had been wearing and walked past Jennifer. He went to the living

106

room, got dressed, and sat on the couch with a loud sigh. The last few minutes played out in his head again. That really had been a cruel thing to say, and it had endangered his only shot at getting home.

"What a piece of work you are," Charles said to himself. He leaned his head back and stared off into the ceiling, trying to figure out what he could do to make everything alright again. His eyes became heavy, but he hardly noticed as they closed. Charles drifted closer and closer to the edge of sleep. Something touching his face jerked him back to consciousness. Jennifer was standing over him, still nude.

"I'm sorry," she said.

"So am I," he replied.

"Look…I don't know if Charlie wants to come home or not, and that hurts a lot. I want to believe he does, but if you belong here and he belongs there, maybe he won't come back to me. That's something I would have to deal with, and if that's the case, I won't mind dealing with it with you. That's all I can say. I'm not in love with you, but I don't know what the future has in mind. Obviously, stranger things have happened."

Charles didn't know what to say. He just smiled and nodded. She held out her hand and pulled him to his feet when he took it.

"Now, let's get this ritual done and see what happens," she said.

"Should I get naked again?" Charles asked, laughing a bit.

"Of course," Jennifer said.

"And then what?" Charles asked as he followed Jennifer back to the bedroom.

"Then I want you to sit cross-legged on the floor across from me with the quartz between us. I'm going to guide you through this meditation, and I'm hoping that it will have the same effect it did on Charlie. The point is to get you in the right mindset, and keep you there...until...you know."

"Got it," said Charles. He took his clothes off and did as Jennifer instructed, sitting with his legs crossed and his back to the bed, leaving the big chunk of quarts between them. The light from the candles flickered across its faces and little glints of light bounced inside of it. To Charles, it was enchanting. He didn't know the reason for the crystal, but just staring at it was already having a calming effect on him.

"Let's start with your breathing. Straighten your back and breathe in through your nose until your lungs are full. Do that slowly then exhale through your mouth. Close your eyes after you have a solid rhythm, then I will count us down."

"Count us down to what?"

"To a meditative state. Think of it like hypnosis."

"Got it." Charles began to breathe as Jennifer had told him. He waited for the countdown to start as a feeling of light-headedness came on. He closed his eyes and felt himself drifting, not to sleep, but into a relaxed state.

"Now, I want you to visualize the count as we go through it," Jennifer said. Her voice was soft and seemed far away, but Charles understood just fine.

"One..."

Charles imagined a black number one against a white background.

"Two..."

The number changed without Charles having to expend any effort.

108

"Three…four…five…"

Charles could feel himself drifting again, but he seemed to have a deeper understanding that it was okay. The feeling became almost comforting to him.

"Six…seven…eight…"

He could no longer feel his body. There was only the numbers, Jennifer's voice, and the sensation of floating away.

"Nine…ten…eleven…"

The only thing that was holding him from drifting away completely was the count. He didn't know how long it was going to go, but he wanted it over. It was like a string holding a balloon back from flying upwards into the air. All that was needed was to loosen the grip a bit and…

"Twelve"

Charles watched the number on the white background fade from his sight and in its place was a deep, impenetrable nothingness. On occasion he would have a dream of flying and awaken with that sensation fresh in his mind. This was the same feeling but intensified.

"Can you hear me, Charles?" Jennifer asked. He could barely hear her voice, but it was there.

"Yes," he said. His own voice surprised him a bit as it was smooth and relaxed. It was as if he was hearing it from outside his own body, like a recording being played back.

"I want you to find a point of light. I'm already there, waiting for you. Find it and go towards it." He turned in the void and scanned every part of it. He caught sight of the pinprick of light and willed himself towards it. It grew larger in his vision and he had the strangest sense that it was pulling him as he pushed towards it.

"Good. I can see you on the other side. Come through it. It should be easy for you." Charles stopped pushing and the light, which was quickly becoming a hole, guided him towards it. At first he thought that it was too bright; that the light that came from within would blind him. But as he approached the threshold, he felt its warmth and his fears melted away.

He could see Jennifer on the other side. She was a simple outline, but he knew it was her. She held out a hand and he reached through to grab it. Her grasp was light; it was as if nothing was there at all. Then, he was through.

"Where are we?" Charles asked.

"We are on the astral plane. But now that you are here, we have to find the edge as Charlie and I did," Jennifer replied.

"Where is the edge?"

"There," Jennifer said, pointing upward from where the two of them floated. All he could see was more white light, but he knew there was something else. He could actually feel something enormous looming above them. As he stared, it all came into focus. Behind the white were swirls of blues and reds. They were faint, but they were there. Déjà vu took over.

"I've been here before. I've seen all of this before. That edge swallowed me in a dream," he said.

"It was no dream. That was you being propelled into it. It may have seemed like it took you, but it was actually you being forced towards it by Charlie ejecting you."

"Then, it was on purpose?"

"I don't know," Jennifer said in a solemn tone.

"And I have to go there again? It terrified me the first time. It was like what I have always imagined drowning feels like."

"I believe that it will open to you and it will be your own will that moves you through it. Nothing about it will be involuntary. If all goes according to plan, you should end up exactly where you need to be as long as you keep that destination clear in your mind."

"So, this isn't a for sure thing?"

"It's as close to sure as I can get."

"Okay. Take me there."

The two of them, hand in hand, flew up to the edge of the astral plane. There was no sensation of being forced one way or another, and that put Charles's mind at ease. He began to wonder exactly what was beyond the edge, but stopped when he realized that he didn't have any frame of reference to form a right answer. To him, it seemed as if it was the surface of the ocean, and beyond it was open air. But if that were true, then beyond the open air would be another ocean, and he knew that wasn't true.

Charles and Jennifer stopped at the edge.

"Okay. This is where we part ways," she said.

"Right. You have to go back and—"

"Screw your semi-comatose body, yes," she said, giggling a bit.

"I really am sorry for before."

"I know you are. I can't imagine what you were seeing and smelling and tasting in my world. I can only assume that your feelings were just as intense."

"I'll find Charlie. I promise."

"I know you will. But, on the off chance you wake up next to me, I guess it won't be that bad." Charles didn't say anything to that. A part of him wanted to stay there, and a part of him wanted his own life back. He supposed it wouldn't be that bad to wake up next to her either, but he said nothing. Instead, he reached out and hugged her. Again, it felt as if there could have been nothing there at all, but he knew there was, and that was enough.

Charles let go of Jennifer and she flew back down to the threshold. He turned back to the edge and examined the part of it in front of him. It really did look beautiful on the other side. If he hadn't already gone through all of the highs and lows of the day and come to accept that all of this was really happening, he could see how it would seem as if it was a dream. But, it wasn't. Everything Jennifer had said was true, and he would remember it all for the rest of his life, no matter where that life ended up being led.

Floating there and musing on the beautiful colors swirling in front of him, Charles felt a wave of pleasure come over him. It made his entire body tingle and he immediately knew what it was. Back there in the physical reality, Jennifer was finishing off the last part of the whole sordid affair. As the pleasure rolled over him, the colors beyond the edge became brighter and more intense. The entire edge seemed to be humming, but Charles realized that it wasn't the edge at all. It was him.

With each torrent of exhilaration, Charles fell into time with the edge. He thought hard about where it would take him. He thought about his Jennifer. He thought about his home and his job. He thought about Charlie. Then, his very being seemed to tense up and become completely relaxed all at once. For him, the edge disappeared. With all of his thought of home projected firmly within his mind's eye, Charles floated forward into the unknown between worlds.

For a time, Charles was nothing but a wave. Then, he was nothing but his senses. He was nothing, something, and everything, all at once. But his mind kept repeating the same images.

Jennifer
Charlie
Home

He sped through the edge, seeing everything as vivid liquids crashing into each other, then as vapors intertwined in visions of beauty. There were shapes that held no shape at all. He stretched out over leagues, racing towards the things he kept his focus upon.

Jennifer

Charlie

Home

He saw the beautiful interplay of form and substance give way before him. It all parted and all was white on the other side. That was his place. The threshold that led to his life was on the other side of the tunnels that swirled around him. But he was not there yet. He concentrated.

Jennifer

Charlie

Home

Then, all at once, the far end of him caught up with the front and Charles burst though the edge, leaving the swirling madness behind him. Everything felt familiar to him, even though he had never consciously been here. He knew this part of the astral plane, because he had always been just out of reach of it. But there was no time for sentimentality. He had to find the threshold that led to his life and to Charlie.

Charles flew about the astral plane, and after what seemed like a very long time, he spotted a dark hole far below him and far from the edge where he had come out. It was his, and he knew it. Charles raced towards it, and as he got closer, he saw that he was not alone. Floating next to it was another form. Like Jennifer, it was just an outline, but he knew what it was. The only thing it could be.

"Charlie, I presume," Charles said, coming to a stop in front of the threshold.

"And you're Charles. I've been waiting," Charlie said.

"So, you knew I was going to come and take my life back?" said Charles. His tone surprised even him.

"Well, I knew you were going to come, but I don't know about taking your life back. See, you have what I was supposed to have, just as I have what you were supposed to have."

"Yeah. Jennifer figured all of that out. What you aren't taking into account is that I don't care. You stole my life, and I want it back."

"Do you?" Charlie asked.

"Of course I do!"

"Are you sure? Or is it just that you are so familiar with your life that the prospect of something so new and fantastic has you scared? I'm sure you noticed the differences between the two."

"There are no differences. Our worlds are the same in every way except for, as far as I can tell, us."

"I don't mean the worlds themselves. I mean the sensations. The colors are brighter. The air is sweeter. Everything seems just a little more…right. You had to have noticed it."

"Yes, I did."

"So, you see. Even the cosmos know that going back is a bad idea."

"I don't care what knows it's a bad idea. You stole my life, my home, and my girlfriend. I can't let that go."

"Can't you? Think of it like this: If your car is totaled and you have great insurance, you get a new car. Sure, it doesn't have the indent in the seat that you have made with your ass, or the radio programmed to the stations you like, but it has that new car smell and feeling to it. Eventually that passes, but you don't even notice. Instead, you become comfortable and day after day it becomes yours."

114

"I don't care. Jennifer misses you, and I miss my girlfriend."

"Fiancé, now."

"You…you proposed?"

"I had to do something. She was wondering why I was so nervous in the morning. I found the ring and figured you were going to do it anyway, so I bit the bullet. It got her out of the house and shopping all day while I adjusted."

"I was going to propose after I got the VP position!"

"Yeah. I figured that out. Look man, I have to ask this, because I've had some insight to your life and I really need to know, as much as I think you need to be asked. Are you really happy there with your Jennifer? Really, truly happy?"

"Of course I am!"

"Because it seems like you have simply led a carefully planned life based on nothing but ambition and ladder-climbing. I mean, what kind of life is that? Granted, you have the things that I wanted so desperately for myself and for Jennifer, but you seemed to have sucked all the joy and adventure out of life to get there. So, I ask you again, are you happy there?"

"Y-yes. I am. My life is great."

"Is it?"

"Yes!"

"And there is no way that you would want to go back to my Jennifer and our tiny apartment, permanently remove the metal rod up your ass, and live that way?"

"N-no…"

"Are you sure?"

***

115

Charles woke up. His eyes adjusted to the first rays of sunlight coming in from the bedroom window as he stared at the ceiling. He turned on the pillow and looked at Jennifer sleeping soundly next to him. He smiled and fell back asleep.

RETURN

On the day they arrived, Devon's father killed himself. Being a man of faith, nobody saw it coming, but the revelation that the faith he had held on to so dearly was all a lie pushed him over the edge. When one's reality is shattered so completely, picking up the pieces seems trite. So, that evening, Devon's father went upstairs to the room he shared with his wife, took out the gun he kept "just in case", and blew his brains all over the wall above the bed he had slept in for 22 years.

Had anyone been home, they would have heard it and known that the man of faith they called husband and father didn't die when they began purging the planet. They would have known he was spared the terror and sorrow. This may have brought Devon and his family a bit of peace in the time ahead, but there was no such luck. They said the first city to be hit was Hong Kong, but the first casualty after the things appeared was Devon's father, a fact nobody would ever know.

There wasn't a soul on Earth that didn't hear the broadcast when it came. It came through clearly on every television, cell phone, mp3 player, car stereo, and computer in the world. Nobody understood it, of course, but after ten minutes or so of what sounded like garbage, a piece of the broadcast was translated. The message was on a loop and most of it was undecipherable. One phrase, however, was clear.

"What are you?"

Instantly, there were people preparing responses across the globe. Linguists and scholars put together greetings for the leaders of every country. There was no unified global effort, although it was said that America tried, wanting to put

117

the President out in front of the entire thing. It's also said that not one country backed him.

Japan was the first to transmit.

"Greetings from the planet Earth. We are humans, the most advanced race on our planet. We welcome you and honor you."

A few seconds later, the rest of the world transmitted their messages. Some sent greetings from their own countries, while others, like Japan, came on as ambassadors to the entire planet. The response, however, was not so varied. A voice spoke in distorted and broken English.

"Judgment to come."

Nobody knew what to make of it. In Devon's household, his father told them to pray, because that's what they did in times like these.

"God has a plan," said Devon's father. Devon couldn't understand what the plan could be, but was also taught to never question it. That wasn't the way of the devout. You had to have faith.

Hours later, another transmission crackled through the airwaves. This time the language was perfect.

"Judgment has been passed. We will preserve the biological race memory of the species for study and sanitize the planet for use in further experiments. Mutation of Species 879-A is classified as genetically unstable. Sanitization will commence shortly."

Devon hung on every word that came through in that horrible voice. He looked over at his family, tears filling their eyes. Devon's father put his head in his hands. After a long silence and dead air, the President came on the screen. Nobody was listening. The words of one man held no longer held weight. The human race had been judged, and not by the hand of God, but by things from another world.

118

After a while, Devon's father spoke. He told them all to pack light and head to the church while he had locked down the house and would be right behind them. He never came.

Inside the church people had gathered around a television that had been brought in. The world was attempting more communication with the beings, but to no avail. Their words were falling on deaf ears. A scientist came on at one point and said that it was no surprise that humans could have come from some kind of primordial leftovers, a byproduct of some grand experiment conducted by these beings. At that, the pastor shut the television off.

"God has a plan," he told his congregation. Devon still couldn't see what it was, and began to wonder if questioning God's plan could help him understand. The pastor continued.

"With everything we have left in us, we have to have faith that the Lord will guide us and keep us from harm. We have to have faith that humanity will continue on, and that these things that seek to deceive us into believing we are nothing more than an accident will be driven off by the power of our faith."

Devon raised his hand. The pastor looked at him, acknowledging he had something to say.

"What is our biological race memory?" he asked. The pastor frowned at him.

"I don't know any more about that then you do." Devon furrowed his brow. The question came out of him reflexively.

"Is it God?" Everyone fell silent and stared at Devon.

"Are you asking me if these things intend to take our divinity?" the pastor asked. Devon wasn't sure what he was asking, and he knew that this line of thinking wasn't going to go anywhere. There were just too many questions to ask, and nobody had the answers except God. God and the things poised to "sanitize" the Earth.

The television could have told them of what was happening in the outside world, but it remained off. Out there, beyond the huge oak doors of the church, people were beginning to be taken. The greatest minds across the globe were vanishing. The best and brightest, those few who had reached the apex of their fields were the first to go. The small groups of people huddled together in the church were unaware that the fate of humanity had been set by things entirely inhuman.

It wasn't until hours later that someone turned on the television. That's how Devon learned of Hong Kong. It had been vaporized. Not in the sense of destruction and death littering their streets, for that would have required things to still be there. It had turned to dust. They also learned that the force responsible for the devastation was making its way West. Nothing was left in its wake. Only dust.

The scale of it all sent some into shock. Others felt nothing but outrage. Devon began to feel numb towards all of it. Maybe it was that he still hadn't accepted that it was really happening, or maybe some little part of him clung to those four words.

God has a plan.

It rang out in his head, as if to stand against the things happening out there. Was it faith? Maybe, but hope was the more appropriate choice. He had hope that the human race wouldn't be swept away like dust. He hoped that there was some kind of cosmic failsafe primed and ready to put a stop to everything that had happened so far. Devon hoped, but did he have faith? No, he wouldn't have called it that. Not anymore.

Devon's mother asked him if he had heard from his father. Of course he hadn't, but nobody knew that by that time he was already dead in his bedroom, the blood and viscera on the wall already dry. The conversation between Devon and his mother was cut short as another newscaster came on describing what had happened in China, India, Russia, and a laundry list of other countries. It was the same all over. Dust. No bodies left to bury.

The only tidbit of additional information was that people were being taken. They just vanished in a flash of blue light. This could not be proven, however, since any witnesses had been completely vaporized. Any technology had been eliminated that could have recorded such an event. Nobody knew if it was true or a product of mass hysteria, but they pointed out that the things had announced that they wished to study something of humanity. The other opinion, however, became the popular one.

"You see, brothers and sisters?! The Rapture is upon us!" cried the pastor. Devon couldn't believe what he was hearing. The middle aged preacher was equating being rounded up like some kind of test animals while the rest of the species was snuffed out to the supernatural "life boat" described in the bible.

Devon knew the concept well enough. Before the Apocalypse there would be a time when the faithful would be rewarded and saved as to not have to suffer through the age to come. Devon knew that this was not the Rapture, but with each broadcast it became clear that this *was* the end.

Some of the people began to pray out loud for the Rapture to come to them. Some bargained for their own lives while others begged and pleaded for their families. Everyone wanted something. Devon began to understand why God never answered prayers. These people couldn't help themselves, why should the burden of making everyone's life nice and rosy fall on Him?

On the television, riots had begun to break out all over the globe. The sense of hopelessness in the masses had turned into outrage and anger. There was nothing anyone could do to save themselves, not really. Devon knew this because no matter how hard the congregation surrounding him prayed, nobody was going anywhere. The pastor spoke again.

"Brothers and sisters, this is the time for rejoicing, not sorrow and tears." Devon had an idea what came next, but never truly thought it could happen. Nobody could have been so sure of their faith that they would claim to know the way to paradise. "For those that wish to receive the Lord in Heaven above instead of here on Earth, I can offer you salvation." He pulled the gun from behind the pulpit.

Some people screamed, like Devon's mother and sisters. Not Devon though. He knew that there was a sick logic to it in the pastor's head. He wouldn't hurt anyone unless they asked. They couldn't kill themselves; that would guarantee a one way ticket downstairs. But the pastor could "save" whoever wished to be "saved", and if it was an act of mercy and faith, his sins would be absolved. Devon laughed, not because he found it foolish and ignorant, but because he had figured it out. He knew the rules of dogma. His father would have been proud to know that his son had listened.

Half a dozen people lined up to receive the pastor's "blessing". Devon's mother looked away, but Devon kept a close watch, hoping to catch a glimpse of the souls leaving the bodies. With each thunderous clap from the gun, the pastor yelled out a "halleluiah". Devon's mother just screamed. Devon watched, but there was no sign of any souls. When it was over, the pastor dropped the gun, fell to his knees, and prayed in silence.

Nobody spoke for a while after that. There was only the television, still reporting on the end of the human race. Everywhere, people were trying to fight an enemy that regarded them as nothing at all. When all of Europe and Africa were gone, Devon broke the silence.

"Pastor, would you like me to shoot you?" he asked. The pastor raised his head and looked at Devon.

"Son, that would be murder," he replied.

"It would be the same as what you did, except I don't care about having that sin on my soul. I am going to die, like everyone else here. Like the people you just killed. I can save you pastor, because I don't care about being saved anymore."

Everyone in the congregation was listening by then. Devon's mother started to choke up, but Devon just stared at the pastor.

"You would save me, and take that sin upon yourself?" the pastor asked.

"I would, because I don't think it really matters anymore," replied Devon. The television squawked that that the devastation was arriving on the East coast of North America. The United States would soon be overtaken. Neither Devon nor the pastor broke their gaze.

"I will pray for you," said the pastor. Devon reached down and picked up the gun. It was heavier than it looked and felt warm in his hand. The pastor stayed on his knees and prayed. Devon held the gun out in front of him with both hands and leveled it with the back of the pastor's head. The television spoke of the East Coast being turned to dust, the same as everywhere else. No survivors. No communication. Vaporized. Devon fired.

Some screamed while others fell to their knees and rejoiced over the pastor being saved for his "good works". Devon had heard enough about God and his promises. These people would be dead within the hour anyways. There wasn't going to be any world after this. No years of trials and tribulations. No grand and glorious battle for the Earth. There were only those things in the sky and dust.

Devon dropped the gun to the floor and took his position behind the pulpit.

"People, go home. There is not going to be salvation or redemption or Rapture. There is only going to be death. Go home and take your family members with you. Go home and be together when the destruction hits us too. Don't huddle in here like frightened kids. Go be where you want to be. God isn't here."

The assembled people, his family included, marveled at Devon. He stared out at them and knew they understood. As if to signal their exodus, the television spoke of the destruction sweeping through North and South America. They said there was no one left in the world followed quickly by the newscaster blowing his brains out on live television. The congregation gathered their things and moved towards the door. Everyone left, except Devon's family.

"Mom, get out of here. Take the girls and go home. If you're lucky you can catch Dad and…" Devon's mother cut him off.

"We are staying here and waiting for your father. There is no other place I want to be than here, in the place that brought so much joy to the man who brought so much joy to me. Here, with my family." Devon understood.

Suddenly, a wave of nausea passed over Devon. It felt like his head was floating up and his stomach was sinking at the same time. He looked out at his family, their faces frozen in expressions of awe. A blue light came into view at the edges of his vision and Devon began to feel warm.

"Mom?" he asked. Her eyes were filled with tears and a smile crossed her face.

"God has a plan," she said. The blue light enveloped Devon and he felt himself pulled away. Not long after, the church where his mother and sisters had waited for his father was gone. But Devon was not, no matter how much he wished he was.

***

It was really a simple idea. Take the best and brightest, then take specimens by region, and finally take a set number of randomized specimens to measure variables. It would give them everything they needed to catalog humanity. The specimens themselves were useless, but the knowledge inside of them would be preserved. Devon equated it to throwing away the shell of a peanut after you have cracked it open and gotten to the good part.

To Devon, it was less like being sedated and more like being hypnotized. He still stood in line with all of the other people and shuffled along as the line advanced. He didn't care to run, nor did he feel the fear that would trigger such a response. He felt blank, as if there was nothing wrong with what was happening.

He could see the procedures happening ahead as he moved forward. Robotic arms strapped people down to a metal table and inserted what looked like a large needle into the top of the head. About a minute later, the person was dead and the table pitched forward, sliding the corpse into a hole in the grated floor. Devon figured it was a disposal method of some kind. He knew he should feel something, but nothing came to him.

Devon's turn on the table was approaching rapidly. He had no reservations about it. He didn't particularly want to die, but there was nothing he could do. Where would he go? His planet was wiped of all life, and what remained of humanity was having their grey matter removed and stored away. There was nowhere to go and nobody to turn to.

Then, Devon remembered his mother and how happy she had looked as he had been taken. She believed that God had come to save her son, and she died with that belief. Her and his sisters had been vaporized thinking that he was in the presence of the divine and away from the wave of destruction that came for them. Devon wondered if his father had ever made it to the church. He hoped so, and in that, Devon felt something for the first time since arriving on the massive ship stationed above the now dead rock once known as Earth. He felt hope. The belief in something that he couldn't ever know for sure made him happy. Devon understood.

Two people stood in front of Devon, a man and a woman. The man stepped forward and his procedure began. Devon tapped on the shoulder of the woman in front of him. She turned around with a blank expression on her face.

"It's okay," he said. The woman looked puzzled at the statement and turned back around. The man that had stood in front of her was dumped and she stepped forward. Her procedure began. Devon smiled as the needle was inserted and everything she had ever been was uploaded.

It was Devon's turn. He lay down on the table and could see what looked like a camera right above him. Devon looked into it and smiled.

"God has a plan," he said. The robotic arm stuck the needle into Devon's brain.

THE HERMIT

Gerald waited at the bus stop for the first time in decades. He had always driven himself, trying to keep his solitude complete, but with his car in the shop, there was no choice. He had to get to work as quickly as possible. More than that, he had to have as little interaction with people as possible. Talking to others would be more than devastating after years of careful movements and quiet living. It would ruin the purpose of his self-imposed exile.

The bus rumbled down the block, snapping Gerald from his own thoughts and into the vivid daylight of the world around him. It groaned to a stop in front of him and the driver opened the doors. Gerald picked up his tan briefcase and let go of the street lamp he had been leaning on. His left hand immediately hurt, and Gerald realized he must have been gripping it tighter than he had realized. His nerves were already wrecked, and he still had miles to go.

Gerald almost fainted upon seeing that there was no unoccupied seat on the entire bus. 'Just my luck' he thought to himself. He paid his fare and began to move down the aisle, hoping to find somewhere to sit alone. The only spot unoccupied was next to a young man in a white shirt and blue tie. At the young man's side sat a black leather briefcase. Gerald gathered he was some kind of young professional, and although that shook him to the core, he sat down next to the young man averting his gaze as he did so.

The young man looked over at Gerald and smiled, but Gerald didn't notice. He was determined to not make eye contact with anyone.

"Not a bad day for a broken down car, right?" asked the young man. Gerald froze. How did the young man know his car was broken down? Panic set in. "Yeah, it broke down a few days ago, and they say I probably won't have it back for at least a week. I could have gotten a rental in the meantime, but this gives me a chance to relax on my way to wherever I'm going. Today, it's Ashbury Innovations. Job interview."

Gerald heard the man say 'Ashbury Innovations' and all the tension that had built up since this morning floated away. For a moment, Gerald wondered how the entire chance encounter had come together. His mind began doing the math, calculating the probability of being next to this man at this moment. He stopped himself when it got into the millions and looked up at the young man.

"That's a pretty successful company, kid. You think you have the knowledge and the drive to get the job?" Gerald asked. The young man smiled in a sly fashion.

"I think so. I mean, the guy who founded it wasn't much older than me when he did so. Who says I can't get in and work my way up from Statistical Analyst to CEO one day?"

"True enough. I hear the CEO is a bit of a recluse. No photos of him, no phone number, not even an address on record," said Gerald. "Some kind of modern day hermit."

"I heard the same. Reporters have been trying to find him for years. Even his Board of Directors has never met him. Guess he erased himself completely," replied the young man.

"Think about everything that company has done for the world. Genetic engineering, cybernetics, space travel. They say the CEO does most of the work himself. If you were a quadrillionaire genius, you'd be a bit eccentric too. Paranoid, even."

"Probably. There's a fine line between genius and crazy, I guess. I'm David, by the way." The young man held his hand out. Gerald took his hand and they shook.

"David, a pleasure to meet you. You're hired."

"Excuse me?" said David. Gerald pulled the stop cord and rose. He dug in his pocket and handed David a card.

"Give them that at the interview," said Gerald, smiling.

The card read 'Gerald Ashbury-Inventor'. The bus stopped and Gerald got off. 'No need to go in today' he thought. 'My business is done'.

THE WITCH OF CEDARTOP WOODS

"The point is that there is a witch that goes up to the top of that hill on the full moon every twenty years or so," said Mike.

"I call bullshit," said Katrina.

"Yeah! Everyone in town can see the top of the hill on a full moon. Shit, we can see it when it's only half-full!" said Ryan.

"I'm telling you, I've heard it from my grandfather, from my uncle Bill, and I've heard those stories since I was a little kid. I had just forgotten about them until my grandpa reminded me the other day," said Mike.

"Yeah, I've heard that too. That's why I call bullshit. If someone were living out in the woods, someone in town would have found them by now. Especially when deer season hits," said Katrina. Mike sighed in exasperation.

"So is that a resounding "no" to going up there this weekend for the full moon?" he asked.

"Oh no, we're going. Only so you will shut up about "The Witch of Cedartop Woods"," said Ryan. Mike glanced around, making sure nobody in the cafeteria was within earshot. The last thing he wanted was to give the other people at school more ammunition against him. He was already thought of as the weird kid, and he knew it well. Nobody had ever beaten him up or bullied him for it, nothing like that. In fact, to Mike, the general avoidance hurt a lot worse.

So many of the kids that grew up in the town of Cedartop had been there since birth, like Mike. They all knew each other, and all of their parents knew each other as well. For Mike, this had been a great thing during elementary school and middle school. It was only when high school started that Mike started to dress differently, listen to different music, and pretty much become a different person than all the other kids who played sports or joined clubs. That was how he got lumped in with Katrina and Ryan, the only other people more avoided or whispered about than himself.

Ryan's family was the only black family in all of Cedartop. That wasn't what had made Ryan an outcast by age 16. Not by a long shot. In fact, Ryan's father had served as the head of the City Council for 8 years until he didn't want to any longer. That's how politics in Cedartop worked. Ryan's family was well liked. His sister was the head of the cheerleading squad and his mother was the veterinarian in town. But Ryan, at age 16, had been in more fights than any other kid. He wasn't a bully by any stretch of the imagination, but he was a hothead. If there was some kind of argument that could somehow be solved without fighting, Ryan would be the first to throw a punch. That was how he attracted the attention of Katrina.

A transplant from Los Angeles, Katrina had no idea how to function in a town like Cedartop. Not only was there no music scene to speak of — unless one called the women's choir that sang each Sunday at church a "scene" — but most of all, there was absolutely nothing for her to do. Katrina instantly stood out against the backdrop of the town. She always wore all black complimented with neon greens and blood reds. Her hair changed color every few weeks, from the electric green when she arrived to a blazing orange to the powder blue it was currently. Black fingernails and black lipstick, every day.

Katrina's mother had moved them here after divorcing her third husband. Katrina's dad had been out of the picture for years, and she sometimes wondered if he gave a damn that she was even alive. Then again, she didn't give a damn if he was, and that usually calmed her. Her mother, a health and wellness "expert" had decided to move to Cedartop when she realized she could open her yoga studio without any competition. Despite being small, the town was not devoid of contact with the outside world, so as soon as her studio opened, the classes filled right up. It made Katrina sick to see the people flock to her mother whereas in L.A. she was just one of hundreds of "specialists". They revered her here. Katrina despised them.

The three found each other fairly easily. Mike and Ryan sat alone in the cafeteria during their lunch period, and Katrina never even showed to lunch. She went outside to smoke a joint, then a cigarette, then came back in to fall asleep in whatever her next class was. The two boys noticed this, and being labeled "violent" and "strange" they figured adding "evil" to the mixture was the next logical step.

When they found her on that first day after school, it was Ryan who had approached her first. He introduced himself and Katrina gave him a prompt "fuck off" and continued on her way home.

"That bitch is fucked in the head, man. I say we leave her be," Ryan told Mike, but Mike was hardly convinced. He approached her next.

"Hey, my friend back there was just trying to be nice," he said, trying to smooth over the situation. Katrina stopped and glared at Mike. He felt himself shrink to mere inches tall.

"I don't like it here. I don't like people. I don't like being harassed on my way home from that shit pile you people call a school, and I do not like people who think they

135

can be my friend," she said. Mike didn't know what to do. He was scared and embarrassed at the same time. Then, as Katrina stood there melting him with the hate rays on full blast, he found the words.

"Okay. Wanna get high?" he asked. It disarmed her immediately.

Katrina had bought a large amount of weed before coming to Cedartop, not knowing when she would be able to find a hook-up in town. Mike and Ryan *were* the hook-up. There was no business end of the whole thing. Mike just grew a few plants just past the edge of the woods, and he smoked with Ryan after school. None of the other kids at school had ever asked him about weed, and he never said anything. As far as the town of Cedartop was concerned, they were drug-free, and that's how Mike wanted to keep it.

It was a leap, but he made it, and it paid off. Within the hour, all three of them were hanging out in Mike's basement getting stoned. They all traded their respective stories and the boys gave Katrina the rundown of how Cedartop worked. Small town with small town values that were so predictable, anything could go on right under their noses if one knew what one was doing.

After that day, the three were together as much as they could be. They were the only outcasts in the entire town, so they had to watch each other's backs. Not that anyone would mess with them, but the principle still stood.

Then Mike started talking about the witch.

"So, it's settled. Tomorrow night is the full moon. Pack enough stuff to keep us occupied. Although, if this story is real, we may be—"

"Dead is the word you're looking for there. How many times have you seen the "teenagers looking for something spooky in the woods" movie before? They die every time. Is that what you want Mike? You want us all dead?" she asked. Ryan and Mike just stared at her looking for any sign that she was not serious. It came as a smile crept across her face. "Goddamn you two are gullible!" she said.

"Yeah, okay Miss Hollywood. Just make sure you're out of the house by seven so we can bake before we head up there," said Mike. The bell rang for third period and the three got up from their table.

"You two going to class, or getting out?" Ryan asked.

"I'm going. Art project to finish up," said Katrina.

"I'm headed out. Care to join me?" Mike asked holding out his arm for Ryan to take it. Ryan shoved him.

"Fag. Let's get outta here," said Ryan.

2

It was after seven and the three were in Mike's basement, a place they had come to know as his "dungeon", and all of them were as stoned as they could get.

"Can we get moving now? I feel like if I sit here, I'm going to become one with your inflatable chair," said Katrina. The boys laughed, but agreed that they should get moving.

Nobody paid any attention to the trio as they walked towards the edge of town. All of them had come to expect that exact behavior out of the locals, and it was what they were counting on. Nobody would phone their parents or yell at them about curfew if they saw them because nobody wanted to see them. Each one had grown to like it, but they never talked about it. They all just knew.

The edge of the woods was serene. People went jogging along the few trails that were visible, but the trio stayed clear of those. The hill was well off the beaten path, but they didn't want to take the chance of anyone seeing them climbing it in the twilight. The last thing any of them needed was to have the sheriff escort them back home, or worse, find any drugs on them. That was a stigma they wouldn't be able to survive in such a small town.

The woods got thicker the closer to the hill they got. The sun was setting fast, casting its fading light between the trees in small glimpses. Not long after, they emerged from the deep woods and found themselves at the foot of the hill as the sky turned a deep violet.

"Let's set up down here. It will be easier than, you know, climbing," said Mike.

"If you were going to make me climb up there, I was going to kick you in the balls," Katrina said, dropping her bag.

"So, did you want to set up the tent now, or did you have something else in mind?" Ryan asked. The other two looked at him, knowing exactly what he was talking about. Katrina pulled out the electric lamp and Mike rolled a joint by its pale blue light. The three of them sat and smoked it, all the while watching for the full moon to rise.

"So, if there is a witch, what do we do?" Ryan asked.

"We shut the fuck up and do our damndest to not be seen," said Katrina.

"And record it on my phone," Mike added.

"And if there isn't anything, then we came out to the woods to sit around all night and get stoned. Because that's exactly what I wanted to do with my evening," said Katrina.

"As opposed to sit in Mike's basement and get stoned? I'd take the woods any night," said Ryan. The others agreed.

They all stood and began setting up the tent. Half an hour later, they were inside of it and filling it with smoke, occasionally poking their heads out and looking up the hill. Nothing showed as the sky grew pitch black and the full moon made its appearance.

As they sat and laughed about the trivial things in their life, the three of them felt a sense of camaraderie. They were the outcasts of their small town, but they had each other. There were no secrets and there were no lies. It went unspoken, but there in the tent, the three of them had never felt closer to anyone else in their lives. Witch or no witch, they were all happy to be there.

A sudden gust of wind howled through the trees and made them all jump.

"We are all a bunch of pussies, you guys know that right?" said Mike.

"Well, you guys are," Katrina said, laughing a bit.

"Oh yeah? Well I think it's your turn to stick your head out," Mike replied.

"Yep. I did it last time," Ryan added. Katrina sighed.

"Fine. I want to stretch my legs anyway." She unzipped the tent and got out while Mike started breaking up weed for another joint. A moment later, they heard something hitting the door of the tent. Ryan stuck his head out and saw Katrina standing there, batting at the door and looking up at the hill. Ryan looked to where she was facing and saw what had grabbed her attention. A swirling black mist had collected in front of the moon which had crested the hilltop.

Ryan reached backwards into the tent and motioned for Mike to come to the tent opening.

"What? I'm comfortable, man." Ryan just motioned to him again as the black mist thickened and swirled around itself on the top of the hill. Mike sighed and made his way to the front, joining Ryan. He saw it and went cold.

The mist picked up speed and rose higher, becoming a black cyclone. The three watched this in terror and amazement, unable to move or speak. The cyclone began to close in on itself, shrinking and expanding until it was clear that it was no longer a swirling mist, but a form coalescing from within it.

The moon crept up the hill, framing the entire scene in silver light. It shone through the mist less and less with each passing second as mist became solid. Arms and legs became clearly defined and lost their inky darkness, giving way to pale white skin. Tendrils flowed out from the head, and seemed to all fall at once, leaving only long, black hair in their place. Finally, the mist swirled about and came to rest draped over the person. The mist was gone, and in its place stood a woman in a long black dress.

3

The woman turned and looked right at Mike with glowing, green eyes. His blood ran cold and he felt as if he was going to faint, but her stare kept him locked in place. She was far enough away that she could have been looking at one of the others, or nobody specifically, but Mike knew in his heart that her gaze had fallen squarely on him.

She took a slow step around and walked down the hill, approaching the tent. As she got closer, her eyes dimmed their glow and Mike could make out the woman's face better. She was absolutely gorgeous.

Her wavy black hair hung down past her shoulder, and her pale skin was contrasted by her emerald eyes and lips. If Mark wasn't terrified beyond anything he had ever felt before, he would have thought her the most beautiful woman he had ever seen in his life. But when she got to within ten feet of the tent, the woman began to stumble. She took one more step forward, and her small frame collapsed on the ground.

Nobody moved. The woman lay on the ground, breathing hard. Mike looked over to Ryan and Katrina, hoping that one of them would move first. When they didn't, Mike climbed from the tent and stood up. He looked back again at his friends, hoping they would step up to join him. They didn't. He turned back to the woman on the ground and approached her. His mind told him that there was still time to turn back and run into the woods, but he ignored it with everything he could muster, listening instead to the much smaller voice that told him the woman was hurt. The small voice told him he needed to help her.

Mike reached her and his fear began to lessen as he heard her let out the softest of cries. She wasn't unconscious or in pain. She was sobbing. Mike knelt down next to her.

"Are you okay?" he asked, his voice cracking. The woman looked up and Mike saw her cheeks were streaked with tears falling from her deep, green eyes. It made Mike want to cry himself. Why was such a beautiful creature so sad?

"You have to help me," she said. Her voice was light, with an accent Mike couldn't quite place. "I've been searching for you, Michael. You and your friends must come with me."

"H-how do you know my name?" Mike stammered.

141

"You are the one from the prophecy that is supposed to stop the war in my land, are you not?" the woman asked.

"I don't know what you're talking about, but my name is Mike. Wait, what land? What prophecy? Who are you?!" Mike asked, coming to the realization that something was very wrong about the whole situation.

"I apologize. I am Diantha, and I have been coming to this hill for what would be centuries for you. I have been coming in hopes of finding you, Michael. It was prophesized long ago that a great and terrible darkness would fall across my land, and there would be a human that would become our salvation." Diantha moved to stand, and faltered. Mike's hand shot out to steady her and she grabbed it, her soft pales skin touching his. A tangible spark leapt from her to him, and Mike knew that everything she was saying was the truth.

Mike helped her to her feet and turned to look at his friends who were simply staring in awe.

"Guys, I think she's telling the truth. I don't know how I know it, but she is," he said to them.

"A woman appears out of thin air and tells you that you are supposed to save her, and you believe it?! She's the witch, man!" Ryan yelled.

"I am no witch. I am Fae. Why would you say something as horrible as that to someone you have only just met?" Diantha asked, cocking her head to the side and giving Ryan a look of confusion.

"I don't care what you are. You said you have been coming here for centuries?" Katrina asked.

"Yes. For me, my search only began this morning. But each time I appeared on each full moon on this side, I found nobody was waiting for me as the prophecy had foretold. Until now," she said. Her hand flourished and a scroll appeared from nowhere.

142

"Whoa," said Mike, taking a step back as Diantha unrolled the parchment and cleared her throat.

"It is written that one day, the child of the viridian and the ebon...that's me...shall travel to the world-in-between on a night when that world's sister shows her true face. The child shall bring the knight, a boy-child known as Michael, and his companions to our world. Michael, along with the one of dark skin and the feline, shall stave off the attacks of the sky reptiles, saving the land from certain destruction." Diantha rolled the parchment back up and it disappeared as quickly as it had appeared. "That is the prophecy I speak of. Now, will you come with me? There is no time to waste."

"We have to go, guys!" said Mike. He had believed it before Diantha had read the disappearing scroll, but now his belief was solidified. And if Ryan and Katrina were not going to come with him, he would go alone. He certainly didn't want to go trekking off to some unknown land with a strange woman he had just met, but he saw no other option. He was destined to save her world; he could feel it through and through.

"You aren't actually considering doing this are you?" Katrina asked.

"Yeah," said Mike and Ryan simultaneously. Mike looked over at Ryan, surprised. Ryan shrugged.

"I'm not going to let you go by yourself. What kind of friend would I be if I did that?" he asked. Mike smiled.

"Goddammit! And I suppose I have to go to make sure you two don't get yourselves killed by...what was it again?" Katrina asked, looking at Diantha.

"Sky reptiles. You call them dragons," she said.

"Dragons. Right. Of course it's dragons. Why wouldn't it be dragons? I mean, it's not like this isn't crazy in the first

143

place, why not just throw some dragons in too?" Katrina said.

"So you're coming?" Mike asked.

"Yeah, I'm coming," said Katrina, obviously displeased. Mike was ecstatic.

"Then it's settled. We need to get back. Join me on the hill and I can open the path back," Diantha said, turning and moving back up the hill. The three friends followed her, looking at each other and smiling. They had come out looking for something fantastic, and had found it. Mike was beside himself with excitement. He wondered if Diantha would fall in love with him after he saved her world and its people. He wasn't sure how he was going to accomplish that, but it didn't matter. The prophecy said he would, and he believed it now as much as Diantha did.

"I want us all to link hands as I open the path. If you let go, you could be lost forever. Do not listen to the things that live between our worlds. They will lie and tempt you to leave the path, but you must not," Diantha said. "Now, link hands and close your eyes. Keep them shut until I tell you to open them, and not a moment before."

The four of them formed a circle and Diantha began to hum in a light and airy tone. Everything seemed to lurch to one side, but Mike stayed standing. He had the sensation that he was moving, but his feet never seemed to leave the ground. He became cold, and then warm. It felt as if it had begun to rain, then it felt like sun was shining on his skin. Mike could hear far off whispers, but ignored them, knowing it was the things Diantha had warned him of. He kept his eyes shut as tight as he could as the far off voices beckoned him to join them. They sounded lovely, promising him pleasures and riches, but he knew it was all a lie to get him to become lost. That was simply not an option. He was chosen

144

to save Diantha and her people, and nothing could deter him from that path.

Mike lost his sense of time. He didn't know if he had been standing there for seconds or hours, but when Diantha finally spoke, it didn't matter.

"We have arrived. Quickly now! We have no time to waste!" she said. Mike opened his eyes and saw that the landscape had truly changed. Instead of standing at the top of the hill in Cedartop woods, he was standing on the outer wall of a high castle. Below, an army was fighting one of the dragons they had captured in a large net. The beast thrashed from side to side, sending the soldiers flying in all directions. Those that held their ground managed to keep the beast subdued, and the rest drove swords into its hide. He could hear its screams of pain and it sent shivers down his spine. Mike had never heard such a sound in his life, and he knew he would never forget it.

"Time is running out! Arm yourselves now!" yelled Diantha. Mike turned and she handed him a sword. It was heavier than he had thought it would be. He took it without hesitation. She moved to Ryan and Katrina and gave them swords as well.

"What the hell am I supposed to do with this?! I can barely hold it!" Katrina cried.

"You're supposed to stop that!" said Diantha, pointing to the sky. The three of them all looked up to see a dragon headed straight at the wall they were standing on, and it didn't look to be changing its course.

Mike looked over at Ryan who readied his sword like a baseball bat, then at Katrina who did the same. He smiled to himself, knowing that with his friends by his side, they could surely defeat a dragon. They were chosen.

145

Two more dragons appeared on either side of the first. They were smaller, but they were coming in much faster than the larger one.

"You can do this! You are the chosen ones who will save us all. Get rid of your fears!" Diantha yelled from behind them. Mike didn't take his gaze off of the creatures. There was now one for each of them. Good, he thought to himself. That would even out the odds.

Just before the beasts were on top of them, a small voice spoke in Mike's head.

"This is crazy," it said to him. "This is all wrong. You don't know what's happening, you have endangered your friends, and now you are about to die."

With that little voice, reality came flooding back to Mike. He was holding a sword on top of a castle in a fairy world about to try and fight a dragon. Nothing about this was right at all. He went to call to Ryan, but it was too late.

The first of the dragons picked up Ryan in his mouth. His screams were cut short when a sickening crunch rang out as the dragon bit through him. Mike turned to Katrina who looked horrified. He dropped his sword and reached for her, but the second dragon was faster. It flew by, snapping her body in its jaws and leaving only her bloody, dismembered legs in place. Now, it was Mike's turn to scream. He turned to see the large one bearing down on him. He felt his bladder let go, and his mind spoke to him again for the last time.

"You're such an idiot," it said. The last thing Mike saw was the dragon's massive teeth before everything went black.

4

Katrina didn't know if she should run, scream, or both. There had never been any doubt in her mind that the whole myth of a witch on the hill was anything but bullshit made up by the people in a small town to scare their kids. But, that's exactly what she was in that moment; just a scared kid in the woods with her two numbskull friends, face to face with a bullshit myth.

The woman at the top of the hill turned and looked at the three of them. From where she stood, Katrina could see the woman's pale face framed by her straight, black hair. She reminded her of Morticia from the Addams Family, but such a familiar image wasn't enough to calm the overwhelming urge to break away from her friends and try to make it back to town and back to her home where she would be safe.

Any hopes of that happening went out the window as the woman began to walk down the hill. Katrina looked over at Ryan and Mike, hoping they would have some idea of what to do. Instead, they were just staring at the woman, their jaws open and eyes wide. They were going to be little to no help. Katrina turned back to the woman, who seemed to float down the hill instead of walk. She stopped a few yards from the tent and bowed her head.

"Good evening," she said, smiling. Katrina noticed her eyes were black, as were her lips. Her eyes were rimmed with dark eye shadow and her pencil thin eyebrows were solid black. If she hadn't been paralyzed with fear, she would have complimented her on her makeup.

"There is no reason to be afraid, children," the woman said.

"A-are you the witch?" Ryan managed to stammer out. The woman giggled a bit.

"No, I'm not a witch," she said. "My name is Diantha, and I am Fae." The three of them stared at the woman, not knowing how to respond to that. "You three really aren't talkative, are you? It's alright. Let me assure you that I mean you no harm at all. This is just where I come every so often to take in the human world. It is quite beautiful in the full moon light, don't you agree?"

"I guess it is," said Katrina.

"Ah, good! I was hoping you weren't all going to stay silent all night. Am I right in assuming you are from the village nearby?" Diantha asked.

"Well, it's called a town, but yeah," Katrina said.

"How fortuitous that you happened to be out here on this particular night! I always wondered why I have never seen any of the people that live there out here."

"Actually, we came out to see…well…you," said Ryan.

"Me? Do the people in your town know of me?"

"Not really. You're kind of a legend," said Mike. "Like, nobody really thinks you're real, so we decided to come out here and see for ourselves."

"They don't think I'm real?" said Diantha, her voice becoming sullen. In that, Katrina saw something. The thought that the people in Cedartop didn't think she was real had really hurt Diantha. She let out a small sob, and Katrina couldn't help but walk over to her and put her hand on her shoulder. She felt a tangible spark when she touched the Fae's cold skin, but didn't pull away.

"It's okay. No matter what the people in town think, we know that you're real now," she said. Diantha looked at her with tears in her eyes and smiled, putting her hand on Katrina's.

"Thank you," she said.

148

"Hey, I doubt most of the people in town think any of *us* are real either, so we understand," said Ryan. Diantha looked at him, puzzled.

"What he means is that we are basically outcasts in town," Katrina said.

"What crime did you commit to be ostracized from your town?" Diantha asked. They all laughed a bit at that.

"We didn't commit any crime. We're just different," said Katrina. "Mike here is a pretty quiet guy, Ryan is a hothead, and I'm just...I..."

"They think she's a witch or something," said Mike. Katrina shot him an angry glare. "What? I'm pretty sure they do."

"Are you a witch?" Diantha asked Katrina.

"No, but sometimes I wish I was. It would at least make life more interesting," she replied.

"Magic is not something to be taken lightly, child. But would you take the chance if you had it?" Diantha asked, turning her back on Mike and Ryan and taking both of Katrina's hands in her own. Katrina didn't know what was happening, but started thinking about the sideways glances and snickers she had endured ever since moving to Cedartop. It pissed her off, but not at the other people. No, she was mad that those little things made her so sad. She had spent years building up her persona of not caring about anything and everything, but no matter how much she wore that on the outside, all the little comments made their way through her carefully constructed armor and buried themselves deep within her, making a home for themselves as they just cut away.

"Yes, I would," Katrina said. Her voice wavered and her friends looked at her, not knowing what the tone in her voice really was. It was that sadness creeping its way out for the first time since she had met them.

"Then it shall be done," Diantha said. She closed her eyes, still holding Katrina's hands, and began to hum a low note that seemed to come from deep within. Katrina could feel Diantha's body hum in time with the note, as were her own hands. The hum moved up her arms and then down into her chest. From there, it moved throughout the rest of her until it reached her head. It made her dizzy at first, but as the hum deepened, Katrina became more and more focused. The shape of things became sharper. Colors were richer. The night sky was a million tiny lights of every different color and size. The world was more beautiful than it had ever been before.

Diantha let go of Katrina's hands and took a step back. Katrina swayed, still entranced with her new perspective, but as the hum subsided within her, she became more focused on the people around her.

"I have imbued your essence with a small piece of my own. A gift for you, but no small gift at all. You can now do things that no other human can do," Diantha said. "Use it wisely."

Katrina looked at Ryan and Mike, smiling with joy. They looked back at her with wide-eyed stares. She could even feel apprehension radiating from them. Katrina's stomach turned at the realization that her friends were scared of her and staring like she was some kind of freak.

"Stop looking at me like that," she said. Mike and Ryan kept staring. Katrina began to get angry. Who were they to be scared of her? She was still herself. She didn't know what Diantha had done to her, but more importantly, *they* didn't know what Diantha had done to her either.

"I said stop looking at me like that!" Katrina yelled. She could feel her anger swell up inside her, becoming white hot at her core. Then, in the blink of an eye, it became something else entirely. The anger gave way to rage.

Katrina looked to Diantha who wore a devious smile.

"What are you going to do about it?" Diantha asked. Katrina turned back to her "friends" and could feel their apprehension turn to terror. It fed her instead of repulsing her. She willed all of it outward at Mike and Ryan.

At first, Katrina's hands became hot. There was a moment of panic as they felt like they were on fire, but before they burst into flames, the power within her leapt forward from her fingertips. It looked like black lighting as it arced through the air and struck the boys square in their chests. They both fell to their knees as Katrina's power ripped through them. When she felt satisfied, Katrina stopped, revealing a hole blown through each of them. They were both dead before they fell over.

"Now, the price," said Diantha. Katrina looked at her, still seething, but calming with every second.

"What do you mean?" Katrina asked.

"Magic comes with a price, my dear. I thought you understood that," Diantha replied in a very matter-of-fact-tone that sat on the edge of sarcastic. Katrina didn't like it at all. Then, she heard a voice in her head, as clearly as she could hear Diantha.

"This isn't you. You have killed Mike and Ryan. Something is very, very wrong here," it said. Katrina knew it was right before it finished speaking. What had she done? What was she now? What price would she pay for killing the two people who meant more to her than anything else in the world? But the clarity of the situation paled in comparison to the fear she felt when the burning began in her head.

It started behind her eyes, but flooded through the rest of her head in seconds. It felt as if the entire inside of her skull was on fire. Katrina couldn't open her eyes, nor could she hear anything. There was only fire and pain and heat. There was a sun inside of her, and there was nothing she could do.

In her last second, Katrina heard the voice in her mind once again.

"Power corrupts you know," it said as Katrina's head was vaporized from the inside out.

5

Ryan broke into a flat out run, leaving Mike and Katrina behind. If they had any sense at all, they would follow him, he was sure of that. But after dodging trees with only the light of the full moon to show him where they were, Ryan soon realized that running may not have been the best idea. He could have at least taken a lamp with him, but he hadn't thought of *anything*, he just reacted. The sight of that woman appearing out of the mist was enough for him to know that there was something wrong with the whole thing. Things like that didn't happen in the real world. He had only come out so he could get high with his friends. It was better than staying at home all night and listening to his father bitch at him for one reason or another. But this had not been in the plan.

Branches bit at Ryan's face and arms, but he managed to avoid all of the larger trees. He didn't know how far ahead the path was, but he had a feeling he was going in the right direction. A scream that could only have been Katrina rang out through the woods and stopped Ryan dead in his tracks. It was followed by a shriek that was not human by any stretch of the imagination. Ryan knew he could easily break down right there and cry, but his instincts told him that if he did, he would be dead within minutes. He started to run again.

The only sounds were his feet thumping against the ground, his labored breath, and his heart beating in his ears. Ryan started to doubt that he was going in the right direction, but he didn't care. He had to get away and find his way back to town somehow. From there, he would wait to see if Mike and Katrina had followed him, even though the scream he had heard made him fear the worst. He shook the thought from his head and kept moving.

Finally, on the verge of exhaustion, Ryan broke through the trees and found the path. He fell to his knees and gasped for air. His head pounded and sweat was stinging his eyes, but he knew he had to get up and keep moving. He was almost home.

Something fell in the dirt just in front of Ryan. It rolled towards him and came to rest as it bumped against his knees. Ryan began to scream as he looked into the cold, dead eyes of Mike's head.

Ryan scrambled backwards as the inhuman shrieking came from above. He looked up and saw a black shadow. He could barely make it out against the night sky, but he could see that it was hovering there, flapping enormous wings and staring at him with red glowing eyes. It shrieked at him again, and this time was so loud that he couldn't help but cover his ears. Then, amidst the shrieking, a voice spoke to him.

"You're already dead, you just don't know it," it said.

"No! I can run!" Ryan screamed.

"Then do it and see where it gets you."

153

Ryan took his hands from his ears, jumped to his feet, and took off down the path. His legs ached and his chest felt as if it would burst, but he kept running. He could hear the things enormous wings beating behind him, but he had to keep going. He knew that he was faster than whatever had appeared on the hill. He knew he would be safe if he could get to town. There was no way he was going to let his friends' deaths go unpunished.

Claws pierced the skin on Ryan's shoulders and he screamed in pain as he was lifted from the ground. He looked up and saw the creature's gnarled face smiling back at him, its jagged teeth dripping with blood.

"You're not as fast as you think you are," the voice said to him. The creature bit into Ryan's throat as it soared off into the night sky.

6

From atop the hill, the woman's eyes shone a brilliant blue. Below, Mike climbed from the tent and stood next to Ryan. They didn't run or react in any way as the woman walked down the hill towards them. She approached each of them in turn, placing a finger on their foreheads. They would close their eyes and when they opened them, all color had been drained away.

"I hope these are appropriate," said a voice from the woods.

"They will do nicely. I always become nervous when the cycle is up, but your little town never ceases to disappoint," the woman said.

"It was hard to convince the girl's mother that this was the only way, but she came around. After that, all it took was Bernard reminding his grandson about the witch of Ceadartop woods, and we knew they would come." A man stepped from the woods a few yards from where Mike, Katrina, and Ryan stood. The woman turned to him and smiled.

"You gave up your own son for this. Your sacrifice does not go unnoticed, I hope you know that," the woman said. Ryan's father shook his head.

"I am not happy with it, but it was his decision to not fall in line with everything our town has to offer."

"He ran. The rest submitted rather quickly, but he ran. His mind was strong enough that I actually lost him for a moment. You should be proud."

"Did he suffer? Did any of them suffer?"

"In all the time your town and I have had this agreement, nobody has asked that. But before I tell you, I have to ask. Do you really want to know the answer to that? Would it matter either way?"

"No, I suppose it wouldn't," said Ryan's father, looking to the ground.

"You have done well. I will return in twenty years as I always do. Until then, your town has my protection and blessing." The woman turned and headed back up the hill, Mike, Katrina, and Ryan following her. Ryan's father watched as the black mist crept to the top and swirled around the four of them. It rose higher, enveloping them from head to toe, and then dispersed, leaving nothing behind.

About the Author

Tyler Hansen currently resides in Saint Paul, Minnesota, the location of quite a few of his stories. He cites his inspirations to write as his daughter Eris, his father Kenneth, and his mother Cynthia. He enjoys feedback from his readers and can be contacted by email (Hansen.tyler.d@gmail.com), Facebook (www.facebook.com/TylerDHansenAuthor), Twitter (@TylerDHansen), and you can follow his blog (tylerdhansen.wordpress.com).

Made in the USA
San Bernardino, CA
10 April 2014